"There's a horse outside," I said. "At the hitching post."

If I hadn't been watching Grandma carefully, I would have missed the brief shadow that crossed her features.

"What kind of horse?" she asked.

I found the question a bit odd, but then, really, what else could she ask.

"A white quarter horse. A fine-looking horse. Quality saddle."

Grandma nodded as she set her knitting aside.

"No one has come to the door?"

"Not that I know of," she said, her brow creased.

"I'll go back out," I said, pushing off the door. "Look around." I knew who the horse belonged to. I just didn't know where the girl was.

"Don't get caught in the storm," she said.

I stopped mid-turn and looked back at her. She was staring into the flames, her expression troubled.

"What storm?"

MEET ME IN 1879

ALSO BY KATHRYN KALEIGH

THE BECQUERELS
Time Travel Romance

Dragon's Blood

Lavender Blue

Champagne Silver

Twilight Frost

Mountbatten Pink

Written in the Wind

Scripted in the Stars

Destined in the Twilight

Promised in the Mist

Trapped in the Melody

Twist of Fate

When the Stars Align

Once in a Blue Moon

Once Upon a Christmas

A Wish Upon a Star

When Lightning Strikes

Storm of Time

Midnight Storm

When the Moon Falls

Stormborn Angel

Time Tempest

The Heart Remembers

A Moment in Time

Moonlight Shadows

Rescued in Time

Falling Through to Forever

MEET ME IN 1879

THE WORTHINGTONS

KATHRYN KALEIGH

MEET ME IN 1879

MIDNIGHT STORM PREVIEW

To learn more about Kathryn Kaleigh, visit

www.kathrynkaleigh.com

Kathryn Kaleigh

1
____

ADAM AUCLAIR

Colorado
Spring 1879

A light spring breeze rustled through the high grass across the prairie, carrying the scent of Douglas fir trees and Whitebark pine. Cottonwood fluff drifted easily on the breeze, casting a haze in the air. It almost looked like it was snowing.

The rugged Rocky Mountain peaks across the valley to the west still wore their white winter caps though there were a few bald spots where the snow had already melted. The sky stretching to forever formed a wall of white clouds to the east, illuminated from the back by the morning sunlight.

The Rock Creek River, normally a gently flowing stream bubbling its way over its bed of rocks and making a leisurely path around half submerged boulders, spilled over its banks from the melting snow. There was still a bit of bubbling, but there was also an urgency to the water as it rushed to make its way downstream to the rivers thirsty for water in the valley below.

An elk lifted her head from the water, then twitched her ears, calling her spindly spotted babies back to her side. Like most young, they did as they were directed, then darted off again.

The naturally dry air carried a dampness from an early morning shower, not so unusual for the month of May.

My wheelbarrow, old and rusty, but sturdy, loaded with fresh hay, rolled silently over the dirt path up to the horse pens. I adjusted my thick leather gloves before I picked up the pitchfork and started tossing hay over the fence to the horses waiting on the other side.

Had two dapple grays in this pen. One mare and a studhorse. In hopes that the mood would strike to make a foal.

The scent of fresh hay mixed with the scent of spruce trees was smooth and yet sharp at the same time. Like clear spring water and fresh turned earth mixed with a fresh minty scent. There was nothing I liked better than morning springtime here in the valley.

Being the oldest of five, I was the only one of us who remembered the journey that got us to this paradise we called home.

The journey had been hell. I clearly remembered crossing rivers that toppled wagons, sweeping people under their currents. Trudging across high grass prairies with snakes lurking at every turn, striking without warning. Yet somehow, ours had been one of the few families that had arrived intact. Me. My four younger siblings and my grandfather.

Our father had been killed in the war and our mother had died shortly thereafter with the birth of Marshall, the youngest.

As soon as word had gotten to our grandparents here in Colorado, Grandpa had traveled all the way to Mississippi to get us and bring us back.

We'd lived here with Grandpa and Grandma since and they had raised us as their own.

I tossed the last of the hay over the fence and pulled a carrot out of my pocket for the mare. Her lips tickled my palm as she greedily ate out of my hand.

My siblings were in school this morning. A tutor, a spinster nearing thirty years old, spent one week a month tutoring my younger siblings. After the week was up, she would return to Whiskey Springs. She came from a large family and one of her brothers always rode out here with her. Her father had escorted her this time and he was still here, catching up with Grandpa. They were out fishing in the river now, rehashing old times or maybe making up stories as they went. Probably both.

This was the first week the tutor had been here since last October and I'd been listening to the protests of my younger siblings for two days. But my grandparents believed in education, so they had no choice. I'd finished my schooling in Northern Virginia, so I was exempt.

Still. The quietness, without their jabbering and squealing, was deafening.

Nothing but the clucking and scratching of chickens and the occasional grunt and squeal of the pigs.

I didn't mind doing all the morning chores myself for a few days. Not if it was for the good of my brothers and sister.

Granted I was an unusual man. My sense of loyalty to my family was boundless.

As long as I had siblings and grandparents to watch after, I would stay here on the ranch and do just that.

I picked up the wheelbarrow and turned it around, back in the direction of the stables. The barn, painted a deep red, was as big as a two-story house. Two doors stood open on both sides, letting the breeze wash through. During the cold winter months, we kept the horses inside and the doors closed for warmth.

It had been a long, cold winter and the fresh air was good for the horses.

It was good for all of us.

The sun shifted, stealing its way from behind the clouds, sending rays of sparkling sunlight through the air.

That's when I saw her.

A young lady, older than my sister, but younger than me, sitting on a solid white quarter horse on the low ridge several yards from here. The ridge that followed along to the right of the road between the house and the stable.

They just stood there. The girl sat astride, wearing pants. Nothing unusual these days. My sister wore pants on a regular basis, especially when she was out riding. She'd forgotten her hat. Or lost it. Either way, I hated to see her fair skin after a hour or so in the hot sun.

I'd never seen this girl before. Not even in town. I would have remembered her. Her long dark wavy hair swirling softly in the breeze, fell loosely around her shoulders. She looked past me with beautiful eyes, framed with dark lashes and those perfectly bow-shaped lips were curved with curiosity.

I dropped the wheelbarrow, the sound echoing with a loud thud.

Pulling off my gloves and tossing them into the wheelbarrow, I took two steps in her direction.

Perhaps she was lost. Whatever the reason, it wasn't safe for her to be out here alone.

Besides the dangers from men alone, there were bears and wolves about, especially this time of year when the bears were coming out of hibernation.

She didn't look like the kind of girl who was prepared to deal with such dangers. She looked delicate. Fragile.

Beautiful.

She tilted her head to the side as I stepped closer, but I didn't think she saw me.

The horse tossed his head in alarm, picked up one foot, then the other. The horse definitely saw me.

She used the reins to hold him in place.

I took one more step.

The cottonwoods were everywhere, blending with the morning rays of the sun and obscuring my vision.

She was standing still, but she was fading. I put a hand over my eyes and squinted toward her.

I stopped and stared right at her, straining to see her.

But she vanished.

2

SYDNEY BRANDT

*S*pring wildflowers littered the prairie as far as the eye could see. And that was saying a lot. The sky stretched forever all the way to the edge of the earth to the south and north. Tall rugged snow-capped mountains met the sky to the west.

White fluffy clouds banked against the mountains. Could be snow, I guess, even in May.

Whiskey Springs Ranch. I was in the right place. The etched wooden sign over the gravel driveway said so.

But the swollen snowmelt river had washed out the bridge. The water must have pushed a fallen tree down the river straight into the bridge. A logical conclusion from the looks of the tree tangled with wood from the bridge. It would bust free soon with the water roaring past, taking everything in its path with it.

White fluff drifted from the cottonwood trees, swirling in the air like snowflakes.

I could see the ranch house from here. A large earth-colored two-story ranch house. Chimneys. A huge deck. What looked like a turret with a column of glass window panes in one corner. Every angle poised to take in the breathtaking views.

A three-car garage attached as what looked like an ambling add-on. Had to be an add-on since the house had been built in the 1800s before garages were even needed.

A faded red two-story barn stood several yards away from the house.

A long winding white fence circling the whole thing. Looked like it was down in some places. Not surprising.

They said the house was deserted. Had been deserted for years.

"How do I get over there?" I asked Mr. White standing next to me.

Mr. White was the closest neighbor to the Whiskey Springs Ranch. The Whiskey Springs sheriff had called ahead. Told him I was coming. Not much help otherwise.

"Won't be driving," he said, chewing on what looked a lot like a pine needle.

I glanced over at him, but he didn't seem to think anything of his comment.

"Any suggestions?" I asked.

"Might be awhile before they get the bridge repaired," he said.

Probably an understatement. "I figured. Any other ideas?" Besides waiting.

"Sure," he said, chewing the pine needle and putting his hands in his back pockets.

I waited, but he didn't answer. An eagle glided through the air, landing in one of the fir trees several yards west of the house.

"Want to tell me?" I asked finally when he seemed to have forgotten the thread of the conversation.

"Take a horse."

I shook my head and blowing out a breath, looked at my rental car, a late model Mercedes four-door sedan.

"Don't have one of those," I said, fighting to keep the impatience out of my voice.

"I could help you out with that," he said.

I turned and looked at him. "Okay."

"You know how to ride?"

"It's been a while, but yes. I can ride."

He nodded. I've got a quarter horse you could borrow.

I studied the swollen, swirling river, spilling over its banks.

"How do I get a horse across the river?"

"That's the easy part," he said with a grin. "There's a good place to cross 'bout a mile down the road."

"The water's cold," I said.

"Horses don't mind so much."

I didn't know how horses felt about cold water.

But I did know that I had to get across this river.

I'd flown two thousand miles to get to the ranch house.

The key was heavy in my pocket as was the responsibility on my shoulders.

I never knew I had an uncle named Jack Auclair and wasn't sure he knew about me, but it didn't matter now.

What did matter was that he had left the house to me. Claimed I was his closest heir. Not possible, but that part didn't matter to the attorneys.

Either way it was my responsibility to figure out what to do with this house and fifteen hundred acres.

3

ADAM

The rest of my day passed in a haze. I finished my chores and by the time my siblings were out of school for their mid-day break, I was on my horse riding out toward the west pasture.

My youngest brother had put a frog in my sister's book bag and her screech echoed through the valley. I smiled to myself. Everything was as it should be, at least on the surface.

I wouldn't admit to anyone that I was looking for the girl I'd seen sitting on a horse not twenty yards from me.

She vanished into thin air. Right in front of me.

And here I was out riding the pastures. Looking for stray calves. Checking the fences.

And if I happened to come across the lovely girl riding a white quarter horse, well, that would just be a bonus.

I shifted my hat lower to keep the sun out of my eyes. The warm sun contrasted with the cool air coming off the mountains. The temperate weather was deceptive though. The sun would burn the skin with no warning at all.

I hadn't told anyone about the girl I'd seen.

There had been rumors about my uncle going a little bit crazy when he was building this house.

He'd built the house for the woman he'd thought he was going to marry.

It was a long story, but he had ended up marrying someone else and they had lived happily-ever-after into old age.

Still. There was that rumor about his questionable sanity for awhile.

I preferred not to be dumped into that particular category.

It was bad enough living out here where people were few and far between.

I'd spent some time in Whiskey Springs. But I hadn't found a woman that I wanted to bring home. I'd all but given up and it was just as well since I had plenty of responsibility to keep me busy with my younger siblings. My grandparents wouldn't be around forever and the responsibility of this ranch and ten thousand acres would fall squarely on my shoulders. It was a lot for one man.

But I had seen the girl on the white horse.

I'd seen her with my own eyes. I was not insane.

The Indians around here would probably call what I'd seen a vision.

It might be true, but I was thirty-one years old and I'd never had a vision. Didn't seem like I'd be starting to have visions now.

It was something else. I was certain of it.

I just didn't know what that something else was.

After I'd ridden the fences for two hours, I decided it was time to return home. It was getting late and besides, I was hungry.

After dinner, my siblings would take care of the evening chores giving me time to go over the accounts.

My grandfather had been giving me more and more responsibility around the ranch. I didn't mind. It was my nature to take care of things. I'd had to for as long as I could remember. I'd been too young to fight in the war, but I hadn't been too young to take care of my mother and younger siblings on the home front.

According to my grandmother, that was why I was the way I was. I'd been molded into a responsible adult from a young age.

As I neared the house, everything was quiet as it should be. I was surprised my siblings weren't out of class yet, but it was first day back after a long winter and the tutor was probably having a hard time getting them back into the right mindset.

I rounded the corner of the house, thinking I would give my horse a good brushing before I went inside the house.

Then I saw the white quarter horse, reins looped securely around the hitching post.

My heart rate increased and I pulled the reins of my horse to a stop.

The horse was here, but the girl wasn't.

I slid off my own horse and looped the reins across the hitching post, leaving my horse next to the white one.

I'd brush the horse later. Right now I had to go inside the house and find the girl.

4

———————

SYDNEY

I took my time riding along the edge of the river. Mr. White assured me, in his noncommittal manner, that I would know where to cross the river when I saw it. I wasn't sure I believed him, but I had no choice, really.

He'd offered to come with me, but I wanted to go alone. I needed time to look. To think. To assess.

Jack Auclair had left me this property. I had no idea what I was supposed to do with it.

I had a busy life in Boston. I was a psychiatrist with a good job in a mental hospital. Not only did I have patients to see and keep track of, I had interns to supervise. Two of them at the moment. They were actually psychology students so I was taking the opportunity to teach them a lot about medications. Couldn't really work in the mental health field without a good solid foundational knowledge of psychotropics.

My parents lived in a retirement community in Florida. They were young. In their fifties, but my father had been a successful neurosurgeon in the military who'd been able to retire at a very young age.

He and Momma played golf, attended charities, and did all

sorts of activities. Just last week, they had attended an art class where they had tried their hand at abstract painting. I think there had been wine involved, but they had downplayed that part.

I hadn't dated anyone in a while. Nearly two years. But I'd been busy. I'd been busy and I'd been burned good and hard. Engaged at twenty-three. Broke up at twenty-five. Now I was twenty-seven and had decided that focusing on my career suited me.

I followed the swollen river until I found a shallow area that looked like a good place to cross.

"Ready, Boy?" I asked the horse, patting him on the neck. His name was Reggie. An atypical name for a horse, but what did I know.

The last time I'd been on a horse was with the ex-fiancé at his family's country home outside of Boston.

He, Richard, had taught me to ride and I'd taken to it like a duck to water.

I guided the horse, Reggie, to the edge of the stream. Let him drink, then nudged into the water. As he took his time crossing, I saw a trout swimming upstream. Amazing.

This was my first time out west and everything was new. The bubbling, swollen stream. The sky that stretched to forever. Trout that swam upstream in ice cold water.

I blew out a breath I hadn't known I was holding when we reached the other side of the river. I hadn't been able to help imagining trees and debris from bridges flowing down the river, knocking over the horse.

I was glad I'd worn a blue jean jacket. The wind coming across the field was chilly, even though the sun on my head was warm. It was an interesting contrast.

There were some dark clouds gathering on the horizon. I patted the key in my pocket. At least I could ride out the storm while I was inside the house.

I'd known ahead of time that the ranch house was big, but as I reached it, I was impressed by just how big it really was.

And the closer I got to it, the more I could see its state of disrepair. There was a cracked window right in front. That couldn't be good. At least it wasn't broken yet. No telling what kind of critters would bed up in the house if they could get through a cracked window.

The paint was most definitely peeling and there were some missing shingles. A broken light fixture on one side of the door. There was a blue spruce next to what I called a turret, but since it started on the ground, it was probably technically called a tower. Either way, it was an impressive feature of the house, one I hadn't seen anywhere else. On a castle maybe.

All the shrubs around the house were dried and brown.

How could anyone let a house like this get into such a state? Why hadn't Jack Auclair sold it long ago to someone who wanted to live here? The best anyone could figure was that he had closed up the house and moved to France. His last known address was France.

Imagine everyone's surprise to learn that he owned a fifteen-hundred acre ranch with a seven thousand square foot house sitting right in the middle of that land in Colorado.

It was unimaginable. He'd just up and abandoned it about twenty years ago.

When everything came out and lawyers did their work, they found my name on a will done ten years ago. Not my parents. Me.

I'd still been in high school when he'd had that will executed. My parents had known nothing of it.

My father had offered to fly up. Go through the house with me, but I hadn't seen the point.

I'd simply put it up for sale and be done with it. Maybe give the money to charity.

But now I was beginning to see the point.

This wasn't just a house.

It was a property.

A property that never should have been abandoned, especially not be left to run down into this kind of condition.

The wind had picked up and tossed my hair across my face. I pushed it away before I slid off the back of the horse.

The first fat drops of rain landed on my sleeves as I tied the reins across a wooden hitching post.

The rumble of thunder in the distance had me hurrying to cross the yard, pulling the key out of my pocket as I walked.

It slid easily into the lock and clicked as I turned it.

I opened the door and stepped inside the house.

5

ADAM

*M*y heart still pounding fast and hard in my chest, I stepped inside the front door, not knowing what to expect.

I heard my brothers talking off to the left back in the room used as a classroom. I kinda felt sorry for the tutor. Her name was Miss Mary Evette. Any sympathy I felt for her was offset by the knowledge I had of her generous compensation. Not only was she paid well, but her room and board were furnished for the week while she was here.

I'd overheard my grandparents talking about having her stay on full time.

It would cost more, but it might be worth it. My sister wouldn't mind, but my brothers would throw a fit. They hated being in the classroom, especially Paul, who at sixteen, claimed to be too old to sit in a schoolroom.

It was funny because Paul spent hours reading and studying on his own through the winter.

If Mary did stay on full time, Paul would have to be released and we'd have to hire on a hand to help with the chores.

I found my grandmother in her sitting room off the main parlor in front of the fireplace, her knitting needles clacking away.

Grandma was always doing something. I was just thankful we had a cook and a housekeeper so she had time to do things she enjoyed. Her and Grandpa both.

She looked up and smiled when I came to the door.

"Did you have a good ride?" she asked. I hadn't told her I was going riding, but nothing got past her. She always knew where we were and what we were doing.

"Yes," I said. "Everything seemed to be in order."

"Good," she said. "There are biscuits in the dining room if you're hungry." She went back to her knitting

"I am. Thank you." I leaned against the door frame. I was always hungry when I came in from work and she knew it.

"What's bothering you?" she asking, looking up, her hands going idle.

"Do we have a visitor?"

"Mary and her father." She went back to knitting, casually dismissing my question.

But I was already shaking my head.

"There's a horse outside," I said. "At the hitching post."

If I hadn't been watching Grandma carefully, I would have missed the brief shadow that crossed her features.

"What kind of horse?" she asked.

I found the question a bit odd, but then, really, what else could she ask.

"A white quarter horse. A fine-looking horse. Quality saddle."

Grandma nodded as she set her knitting aside.

"No one has come to the door?"

"Not that I know of," she said, her brow creased.

"I'll go back out," I said, pushing off the door. "Look

around." I knew who the horse belonged to. I just didn't know where the girl was.

"Don't get caught in the storm," she said.

I stopped mid-turn and looked back at her. She was staring into the flames, her expression troubled.

"What storm?"

6

———

SYDNEY

I made my way inside the house warily. Anything could have boarded up in an old deserted house like this.

Just because I hadn't seen any broken glass didn't mean there wasn't any. It was a big house and I'd be surprised if all the windows had held. Some of them, I noticed, however, must be original. Thick wavy glass that was a lot more durable than modern glass.

It smelled dusty with stale air. Like it needed to be aired out.

A huge stone fireplace was the focal point of the living room. The first thing a person saw when they came into the house. Nice. The first thing people saw when they stepped into my condo was my kitchen.

This was so much better.

I shook my head and went back to focusing on my task of assessing. It was not my job to fall for the charm of a Colorado ranch. I had a career waiting for me back in Boston.

There was still furniture in the house. Someone had at least taken the time to drape a sheet over the sofa and one over the chair, at least.

Nothing else was covered. The oversized wooden coffee table. The matching end tables. The lamps.

I slipped the key back into my pocket and walked up to the fireplace. Rested a hand on one of the sturdy stones. The fireplace, almost big enough for me to step inside, looked well used. The stones needed a good scrubbing to get some of the smut off.

The wind outside was howling around the house now. A deep rumble of thunder echoing from the incoming storm. Surely it wouldn't last long and I could just stay here until it passed.

I wandered over to the tower and looked out. Looking out through the two-foot square window panes, I had a clear view of the storm moving in. It was a fast-moving storm and it was amazing that I was able to watch it as it moved in from the horizon that stretched to forever.

There were no curtains or shades or blinds covering the windows. I couldn't imagine why there would be. There was no one for miles. If I lived here, I'd have an alarm system around the perimeter just in case someone came near and then I'd be free to enjoy the morning sun, the midday sun, and the evening sun. The storms. The snowstorms.

I turned away from the window. I could definitely see the allure.

I needed to take a turn around the house. Go upstairs and look around.

It probably would have been smarter for me to wait until tomorrow. To come out with the realtor. I didn't know what I was looking at. Other than being in awe that I somehow owned this property.

Standing in the middle of the parlor, I closed my eyes and imagined for a moment what it might be like to live here. Why had Uncle jack abandoned the property? Maybe it had been too remote for him and he hadn't been able to find a buyer.

But why me? Why had he skipped over my parents?

My parents didn't even seem to know who he was. It was all very strange.

Raindrops splashed against the window, shoved against the glass by the wind.

I imagined how the wood smoke would smell. Tangy and sharp. Woodsy. The crackling of the flames as they devoured the wood. I heard the faint clicking of knitting needles. Imagined a frontierswoman sitting in front of the fire, knitting socks for her man.

The quaintness of it brought a smile to my lips.

Then I heard the ticking of a clock. It sounded a lot like the grandfather clock we'd had in our home back in Boston. My parents had taken it with them to Florida. Hadn't they?

Then the clock began to toll the hour. I have a very vivid imagination, it's true. But the tolling of the grandfather clock sounded so incredibly real.

I opened my eyes.

The flames in the fireplace were ever so real.

The grandfather clock standing to my right steadily ticked away the minutes. The echo of its tolls still echoing my ears.

A bolt of lightning flashed outside the turret windows and the rumble of thunder crashed all around, seeming to shake the house at its very core.

"I need to sit down."

7

ADAM

"What storm?" I asked my grandmother.

She shrugged and picked up her knitting needles. The steady clacking started again.

And then as though right on cue, I heard a rumble of thunder overhead. It was odd, though, because the sun was shining outside. No rain.

Befuddled, but giving up on my grandmother to be of any further help, I turned around and walked back into the main parlor.

The fire in the fireplace crackled cheerfully, staving off any chill the house might have.

I heard laughter coming from the classroom.

I needed to go outside and check on the white horse. Find the girl who went with her.

But as I turned around, I nearly bumped right into *her*.

She wasn't looking at me. She was just standing there, staring into the fire.

"I need to sit down," she said.

A gentleman to the core, I went into action.

"Here," I said, holding out an arm. "I can—"

She screeched, much like my sister did when she found the frog in her book bag, and jumped a foot off the floor.

I grabbed her elbow to keep her from toppling over.

She swallowed hard as she looked at me. Not exactly the response I had been expecting, much less hoping for.

"Come," I said. "Sit."

She allowed me to silently lead her to sit on the sofa.

I sat across from her and put a name to the scent that she wore. Jasmine. I was certain it was jasmine. Maybe mixed a little with the sweet scent of honeysuckle.

"He isn't real," she said, clasping her hands in front of her and looking past me.

About a hundred different thoughts went through my mind.

The first of them was that *she* wasn't real.

But I had touched her arm and I could attest that she was actually very real. She was wearing denim. Denim pants and a short denim jacket.

We weren't able to keep up with fashion very much out here, but I figured her style, the jacket anyway, came from France. According to my grandmother, that was where most new styles came from.

She was even more beautiful up close than she had been from afar.

Her large beautiful green eyes were framed with lush, thick lashes. But she wasn't meeting my gaze. It was almost as though she couldn't see me...

She must be blind, I decided. That would explain why she hadn't seemed to see me outside either.

"I apologize for startling you," I said.

She shook her head and turned back sharply toward the fire when a log fell in half, sending out a flurry of sparks, some landing on the hearth and others shooting up the chimney.

Blind.

"Are you lost?" I asked.

She turned then and looked right into my eyes.

When her gaze latched onto mine, she seemed to see into my very soul and it nearly took my breath away. Perhaps not blind.

"My name is Adam Auclair," I said, keeping my voice soft like I would with a timid child.

She shook her head again and tore her gaze away from mine.

"You aren't real."

SYDNEY

I closed my eyes again.

But the scent of the wood smoke didn't go away. Nor did the steady ticking of the grandfather clock.

The rain had stopped as suddenly as it had started and the sun was shining brightly.

I opened my eyes again.

The man who called himself Adam Auclair was still there.

"He's not real," I said for the third time.

Maybe if I said it enough, I would be right and he would go away. All this would go away.

This was some kind of trick. My mysterious Uncle Jack was playing some kind of trick on me. I definitely should have waited until tomorrow to come here with the realtor.

Maybe Uncle Jack wasn't really dead or maybe he wasn't even really my uncle.

I opened my handbag enough to peek inside and check my phone service.

None.

Just as I had figured.

Still…

I needed to think.

At twenty-seven and female, I was still within the age-limit of having a psychotic break. Schizophrenia didn't run in my family, but that meant nothing when it came right down it.

I treated schizophrenic patients all the time with no history of mental illness in their families.

The flames in the fireplace were real. The ticking clock was real.

Damn it.

That meant the man was real.

No.

It could mean none of it was real. All or none.

The man—Adam—went to a cabinet and brought back a glass of water. Handed it to me.

I hesitated a moment, but took the small crystal glass from him. No more than a juice glass.

The water was good. I tipped the glass back, finished it off, and handed it back to him.

"More?" he asked.

"Please." I smiled up at him.

As a psychiatrist, I was profoundly good at putting my own emotions aside and focusing on the patient in front of me.

When he smiled back, my heart stuttered.

He was drop-dead handsome. Dark hair, a little too long at the collar of the white shirt tucked into black trousers and tall riding boots.

He had a roguish look about him. But the way he looked at me was intense.

With a nod, he refilled my glass.

"Thank you," I said.

I was feeling a bit better now. A drink of water was a proven technique used to calm someone down.

I supposed it really did work. Even on me.

"Do you know Jack?" I asked. "Jack Auclair?"

"Why are you asking about Jack?" he asked, sitting back across from me and looking at me sideways.

"Do you know him?" Maybe I was getting somewhere after all.

"He was my uncle. He built this house."

My jaw dropped. I tried to do some math, but I couldn't wrap my head around it.

And anyway, my thoughts were dead in the water.

If his uncle was my uncle, then Adam and I were somehow related.

ADAM

"How do you know of my uncle?" I asked.

This girl sitting across from me wasn't old enough to know the man we called Grandpa Jack. Grandpa Jack had been gone even before I was born.

"I don't know him," she said. "But he knew me."

My three brothers and sister were out of school now. I heard their shouts of glee as they spilled into the kitchen on their way out the back door.

"What's all that?" the girl asked.

"My three brothers and one sister. They just got out of class."

"Class," she said, looking toward the fireplace again.

"Yes. They've been cooped up inside all day, so you have to forgive them for wanting to get outside before it gets dark. That and they have chores."

She looked at me a moment, then opened the bag she wore over her shoulder and peeked inside. She had done this once before and she was wearing the same disappointment as the last time she looked inside.

It occurred to me that she might be hungry. She was thin as a rail and probably hadn't eaten for days.

"Are you hungry?" I asked.

She shook her head, a little frown at her brow.

"Have you lost your way?"

"No. I'm here to look at the house. The house and fifteen hundred acres."

"Why fifteen hundred?" I asked.

"Because that's all there is."

"Why not look at the whole ten thousand acres?" I asked, not even knowing what it was we were talking about.

She looked at me sideways.

"What are you doing here?" she asked.

"I live here." When she didn't respond, I continued. "I've lived here my whole life."

"Who lives here with you?" she asked.

"My three brothers and my sister. I'm the oldest. And my grandparents."

"I see." She was staring into the flames again.

"You should meet my grandmother," I said, standing up and holding out a hand.

She pressed a hand against her brow and took a deep breath. Slowly let it out.

Then she opened her eyes and looked at me again.

"Alright," she said, putting her hand in mine.

She was delicate and fragile as a little bird. I led her toward the smaller parlor where my grandmother sat, her knitting needles clicking rhythmically.

The sitting room always had a cozy feel to it. It was smaller than the main parlor, about a third as big and held the heat well. She was sitting under a thick wool quilt with fur on one side for added warmth.

As I stepped through the doorway, the girls hand slid out of mine. I tried to hold tight. But it didn't matter, I couldn't stop her hand from slipping out of my grasp.

I turned quickly, but she had vanished.

I must have made some kind of sound because Grandma set her knitting aside and stood up.

"What is it, Adam?" There was alarm in her voice.

"It's…" I glanced at her, then back toward the parlor. Making a quick decision, I turned and strode to the front door. Threw it open.

Her horse was gone, too.

"Adam," Grandma said, coming up behind me. "Are you okay?"

"No." I said looking into my grandmother's eyes, wise with age. "I think I might be seeing things that aren't there."

10

SYDNEY

I stood in the doorway leading into a smaller sitting room off the main parlor. Rain splashed against the windows and wind howled around the house.

Everything else was quiet. There was no sound of a clock ticking. No crackling flames in the fireplace. No clicking knitting needles and no conversation coming from the other side of the house.

The house smelled dusty and closed off again.

Yet… I could still feel Adam's hand on mine.

As we reached the door, I'd felt my hand slipping from his. I'd tried not to let go, to keep my hold on his hand, but he had slipped away. Vanished.

The sitting room in front of me would have been cozy if not for the cloth covering the sofa and the cold stone hearth.

There were bookcases crammed with thick leather books on the opposite side of the room from the wall of windows. There was a window seat in one corner. With a cushion and blanket, it would be the perfect place to sit and read.

I turned and, going back to the main parlor, folded the sheet aside, and sat down.

I had seen the fire. Felt its warmth and smelled the wood smoke.

The rain pelted against the windows, but the worst of the storm seemed to have moved along taking the thunder with it.

I'd had a conversation with a man named Adam Auclair. It was rather—quite a lot—suspicious that he had the same last name as my Uncle Jack. In fact, he seemed to know of Uncle Jack.

I'd heard the ticking clock. Tasted the water.

So I had hallucinated all five senses.

This was very unusual. Most people favored one hallucinatory sense, two at the most. Tactile hallucinations were rare.

If I were assessing myself, I would ask about stress. I wasn't under any more stress than usual. I didn't think my hallucinations were caused by stress. Nothing traumatic had happened to me.

I clasped my hands together, and rested my chin on them.

Other than inheriting a ranch with hundreds of acres in Colorado from an uncle I had no knowledge of. Even my parents didn't know who Uncle Jack was.

But that wasn't sufficient for a psychotic episode.

It had been fleeting. That was all. It happened.

Being in this old house in this strange place. High elevation and all that.

The storm had moved out and the rain had turned to a steady downfall.

I didn't like the thought of spending the night here.

First of all, there was no electricity. No water.

And second, no cell phone service.

And third… there was something not quite right.

I looked over my shoulder toward the sitting room where Adam's grandmother was supposed to have been.

He wanted me to meet her.

I decided right then that I wasn't going to own a psychotic break. Instead, I was going to blame my environment.

That meant that there was something wrong with this house.

Ghosts.

I shuddered.

If Adam was a ghost, he was nothing like he was supposed to be. He had spoken to me and I had touched his hand. He'd been real. I was certain of it.

When it stopped raining, I decided, I would get out of here. Maybe come back with the realtor. Maybe not.

11

ADAM

"Come," Grandma said. "Sit with me."

Wary and edgy, I did as she asked, sitting on the edge of the sofa next to her.

The warmth from the fire chased away any chill in the room. Grandma had a nice, cozy corner to sit and enjoy some quiet time to herself.

It had not been easy being a grandmother raising five children. But she and Grandpa had done an exemplary job of it and continued to do so. She and Grandpa had taken us in and raised us like we were their own. Being the oldest of five, I'd taken on a lot of responsibility, too, even though they had never asked me to.

Grandma deserved a cozy place to sit, her feet on a little ottoman, and a glass of water on the table next to her.

Besides her knitting, she had a book lying open, face down.

"You saw something besides the horse?" she asked, her voice far too calm.

When I didn't answer, she put a hand over mine.

"Adam," she said. "Who did you see?"

"I saw a girl," I said. "A young lady. About Paul's age." Paul was five years younger than me and two years older than our sister, Angelica.

Grandma nodded knowingly and set her knitting needles and yarn in the basket next to her chair. Seemed she was finished with that for now.

"You talked to her?"

"Yes." Sort of.

"Did you get her name?" she asked.

"No," I said, just now realizing it and feeling so very rude. "I didn't think to."

"It doesn't matter at this point, really," she said. "What was she like?"

"Strange, actually," I said, thinking back to our conversation.

"In what way was she strange?"

"She kept saying 'he's not real.'" I looked to Grandma searching for answers. "It was like she didn't believe I was really there."

"Oh Dear," Grandma said softly.

"What?" I took both her hands in mine. "Please tell me."

"Where is she now?"

"I don't know." I hadn't wanted to tell Grandma this. Hadn't wanted to tell anyone this. But Grandma was being so understanding and I got the sense that she knew what was at the root of all this confusion.

"She vanished," I said. "Her hand slipped out of mine as I led her this way. To meet you."

Grandma picked up the glass pitcher on the end table and, hands shaking a little, filled her glass with water.

"When Grandpa gets back from his fishing trip, he and I need to talk to you."

"Why not now?" I asked. "What are you not telling me?"

"No," she said gently, but firmly. "I won't talk about this

without Grandpa. He had more answers to the questions you're going to have than I do."

I sat back, ran a hand over my face. "Do I need to go outside? To look for her?"

"No," Grandma said. "But I need to see to dinner. See if Frederick needs any help."

Once Grandma made up her mind, there was no dissuading it.

"Of course," I said, standing up and holding out a hand for her.

Tucking her hand in the crook of my arm, I led her out of the sitting room, through the parlor toward the kitchen.

As we passed through the parlor, the grandfather clock began to chime the hour.

And I caught just a whiff of what smelled a lot like jasmine.

12

SYDNEY

There's that saying about men and their best laid plans.

I'd already been a firm believer and after today, I believed it even more.

The rain that followed the storm turned into a soaking, all day rain.

I had enough of an Internet signal to check the weather radar. There was no sign that the rain would be letting up until the middle of the night. And then the rain was going to be followed by snow.

I resigned myself to settling in here at the ranch house until maybe sometime tomorrow. The horse, would be okay. It wasn't the best of conditions, leaving him outside, but it was the best I could do at the moment.

After finding some candles and matches, I lit all of them. It pushed some of the shadows away.

With the rain, darkness was coming in quickly and the house was already spooky enough.

I even found some dried out wood on the porch out back, enough to keep a fire in the fireplace through much of the night. I chose the smaller fireplace in the sitting room, the one where Adams' grandmother was supposed to have been.

Fortunately, it wasn't so cold that I would freeze, but it was definitely cold enough that I was going to need blankets along with that fire in the fireplace.

Taking one of my candles, I headed upstairs to look for blankets.

After reaching the top of the stairs, I quickly got turned around. I didn't need to be up here any longer than necessary, so I found a couple of thick wool blankets and a pillow and took them all back downstairs with me. I had gotten comfortable enough with the downstairs area that I knew I was going to be okay for the night.

I pushed the sofa over next to the fireplace and made myself a bed.

The only thing I didn't have was food and water.

I should have taken Adam up on that offer of food, I thought wryly as I settled onto the sofa, tucking my feet up beneath me and wrapping a blanket over my shoulders.

This was definitely not one of the smartest things I had ever done. But who would have known.

I wondered if Mr. White would come looking for me, but quickly dismissed that as a possibility.

By the time it occurred to me—after my stomach began to rumble with hunger—that I might need to call the sheriff in town, let him know I was stranded out here, my phone had run out of battery. I carried a charger with me, in my handbag even, but since there was no electricity in the house, it along with the phone was worthless.

And being from the city, I hadn't thought it necessary to bring any kind of extra charger devices. Like a portable charger. I didn't even own one, but it would have been easy enough to have bought one and brought it along.

So it was just me and my little fire.

It was okay, I told myself.

I hadn't had any other hallucinations over the past couple of hours, so I had no reason to worry. Right?

I sat very still, listening to the steady rain splashing onto the ground outside. The wind howling around the house. The sound of the fire crackling in the fireplace.

And the silence.

With no electricity, the house had no normal sounds. No refrigerator cycling on. No heat turning on. And definitely no other people moving about.

I couldn't remember ever having felt so very alone in my entire life.

Why on earth would someone want to live out here?

I wouldn't.

Not hundreds of years ago when it was built and not today.

It was too remote.

I preferred the city life. Where I had shopping around every corner. I could get a latte or a sandwich or a sweatshirt. And there were people.

Granted, I spent a lot of time alone in my condo, but there were always people nearby.

I took comfort in that.

But it was for just one night. Just one night I could do anything. Stand on my head if necessary.

I had just closed my eyes when I heard something fall onto the floor upstairs.

13

ADAM

I paced around like a caged man waiting for my grandfather to return from fishing.

My grandmother kept busy in the kitchen, helping Frederick. I wouldn't say she was avoiding me, exactly, but she may as well have been.

She knew I wouldn't try to talk to her about the girl and the horse when anyone else was around, Frederick included.

I went outside anyway and looked around.

Even though I swear I had heard thunder earlier, there was no sign of recent rain. Granted, rain evaporated quickly, but still the ground was dry.

Before leading my own horse to the stable, I looked around to see if I could see any tracks the white horse might have left, but if there were any, they were all mixed in with the tracks of my own horse.

I could track a bear or an elk with no problem, but I'd never been all that good at telling one horse footprint from another. Grandpa could do it, but he was still out fishing.

I brushed my horse, an American paint in white and chestnut, named Traveler. I'd named him after General Lee's horse. My father had been one of General Lee's men in the Army of Northern Virginia, and had held a deep admiration for the general. So when my grandfather gave me this horse, I'd given him the name in honor of both General Lee and my father.

"You spending the night out here?" My brother Paul asked, leading the two dapple grays into the barn.

"Not planning on it," I said, hanging the brush on a hook and giving Traveler a carrot.

"Grandpa just got back from fishing," Adam said. "Looks like they caught a mess of fish."

"Guess we'll be having fish for supper tomorrow then," I said. "since Grandma already made something for tonight."

"Chicken, I think," Adam said, wrinkling his nose.

"Since when do you not like chicken?"

"Anytime I can have fish."

"I get it," I said. "See you inside."

I wanted to go inside, corner Grandpa, and find out what he knew about the girl who had vanished, but I knew he needed time to get cleaned up for dinner. I knew that my conversation with him was going to have to wait until after supper.

So I distracted myself by stopping out back and splitting some wood. I chopped some into kindling since no one seemed to like doing that kind of tedious work. I worked on that until Grandma came out and rang the dinner bell.

Filling my arms with wood and kindling, I went inside to wash up.

I passed Grandpa on the stairs on my way up to my room.

"Sounds like we need to have a conversation," he said, his brow furrowed a bit. He wasn't as good at keeping a straight face as Grandma.

"Yes sir." It seemed to me like he could go ahead and tell me whatever it was he needed to tell me, but apparently this was not one of those brief conversations men could have as they passed on the stairs.

"Come to my study after supper," Grandpa said.

"I will."

"We'll have fish tomorrow," he said over his shoulder as he continued down the stairs. Just like everything was normal.

With a shrug, I continued up to my room. Wasn't going to get anything out of him until after dinner.

Whatever it was they needed to tell me must be serious enough to at least warrant a glass of whiskey.

And whatever it was, I hoped it shed some light on how I was supposed to find the girl I couldn't stop thinking about. The girl who had ridden up to our house on a white horse. She had come inside the house. Stole my heart. Then she vanished.

There had to be an explanation.

And I had to see her again.

How else would I survive since she had my heart?

14

SYDNEY

*I*f this was one of those horror movies where the dumb girl goes outside toward the danger instead of staying inside where it was relatively safe and called for help, then I was the dumb girl.

Stupid. Stupid. Stupid.

I had no way to defend myself. The cast iron candlestick would just make an intruder laugh. But it made me feel better to have something substantial in my hands as I put one hand on the railing and took the first step up.

At least I wasn't wearing a nightgown and high heels.

There was no one here. But I had to admit I hadn't gone in all the rooms upstairs. There could easily be a squatter. Someone needing the shelter.

I didn't necessarily want them to leave, whoever it was, I just wanted them to leave me alone.

But there was no way I was going to be able to get a minute of sleep if I didn't find out where the noise came from.

Maybe a raccoon had come in through a broken window. Assuming there were raccoons out here in the mountains. I hadn't exactly done my research.

In and out. That's what this was supposed to be.

The problems all started with the bridge.

I should have taken that as a sign to go back to my hotel room and wait for the realtor. I didn't know how the realtor would cross the river, but it would have been smart to find out.

I made it up another half a dozen steps.

The house was eerily quiet. Nothing but the quiet rain falling outside to keep me company.

When one of the stairs squeaked, I stopped and stood very still. Listening and looking up into the dark. I expected to see someone step out of the darkness at any minute. A madman. Or maybe a ghost.

My eyes hurt from straining.

Stupid.

I couldn't see past the small circle of light the candle gave off, so it was pointless to even try.

Steeling myself, I hurried the rest of the way upstairs. Just get it over with. Find out what it was and go back down to my warm fire. Get some sleep.

Tomorrow I would be out of here.

Day after tomorrow I would be on a flight back to Boston.

Back to reality.

Reaching the top of the stairs, I looked around a bit before starting my search. Still got a little lost up here, but managed to circle back around to the stairs where I started.

Finding no broken windows, thank God, I started back through the rooms again, making a thorough search. I know I had heard something hit the floor.

I stepped into what someone had made into an office—probably a bedroom a hundred years ago when the house was built—and found the culprit.

A book lay on the floor.

I held the candle up, but saw no evidence of how the book could possibly have gotten pushed to the floor.

Nonetheless, I picked it up and laid it on the desk. Another book lay there on the desk, open.

Pulling out the wooden chair and sitting down, I looked at the writing on the pages.

That's when I realized it was a family Bible. Why would a family Bible be here, open?

I lightly touched one of the pages. It had not been open long. There was no dust. There should have been a coating of dust on the pages. Even the desk had a coating of dust on it.

The paper was old. So thin, it seemed like it would disintegrate with the slightest touch. So I kept my hands to myself.

Holding the candle closer, but being careful not to catch the pages on fire, I started to read.

It was a family tree of sorts. A listing of family members. Births. Marriages. Deaths.

Jack Auclair was at the top. Jack and his wife. Rebecca Becquerel.

So there had been a Jack Auclair way back then.

He and Rebecca had a son, killed in the Civil War. They had children. Before the war, obviously.

Continuing down the page.

One of the son's children was named Adam. Adam Auclair. Adam had four younger siblings.

This was unsettling. Each of the siblings had a spouse. Children. The family tree continued.

Then I saw a name next to Adam's.

Sydney Brandt.

With a gasp, I sat back.

Then looked again.

Sydney Brandt.

I'd never believed in witchcraft. I treated believers in witchcraft with Risperidone. Sometimes Haldol. Those were my psychotropics of choice.

But truly, what kind of witchcraft was this in front of me?

Maybe I needed a dose of psychotropics.

Maybe, at the very least, I had a Xanax in my handbag.

15

ADAM

At some point between when Grandpa got home from fishing and now, Grandpa and Grandma had spoken with each other already and now they were ready to talk to me.

We sat in Grandma's sitting room, leaving the younger ones out in the parlor where they played some kind of parlor game. Cards maybe.

The fireplace was warm and cozy, the flames crackling invitingly. It did nothing to relax me.

Grandpa filled two crystal glasses with the good whiskey. Handed one to me. I rarely got the good whiskey. I rarely got whiskey at all, come to think of it.

I sat in the armchair while Grandpa and Grandma sat side by side on the sofa across from me. Grandpa leaned forward, his eyes on mine.

I took a quick sip of whiskey, then set the glass aside.

I'd never seen Grandpa like this. Not even on the whole trip west across the prairie. And that had been pure hell. The hardest thing I had ever done.

It had been Grandpa's third trip. I don't know how he did it.

He'd gone west with Grandma, then traveled back to West Virginia to get us, then back again with us.

But whatever this was, it was serious.

"I told Grandpa about your… experience," Grandma said.

"Thank you." I nodded. I think. I shifted in my chair. Maybe they were getting ready to take me to the asylum.

"Look," I said. "I'm sure it was nothing more than a trick of the light."

"It wasn't," Grandpa said.

His tone stopped me.

"It was more," he said.

"What was it?"

He downed his whiskey.

"I need to start at the beginning," he said.

I glanced worriedly at Grandma.

"It's okay," she said. "It will all make sense."

Somehow I didn't think it would, but I had no choice other than to listen and let them tell me at their own pace.

"Your uncle, my father, came west and built this house."

"Yes sir," I said. "I know the story."

"But you don't know all of it."

Maybe I knew more than he thought. "He was supposed to marry someone, but married another girl," I said, hoping he would skip everything I knew and get to the part that explained vanishing girls.

"You may not know that he had never met the young lady he was supposed to marry."

"I didn't know that." I still didn't see how it was relevant.

"While he was here, building the house, waiting for her, another woman… appeared in the house."

Appeared. Something about the way he said the word brought a lump to my throat.

"What do you mean?"

"She was like a siren. He forgot all about the woman he was betrothed to. Fell head over heels in love with Rebecca."

"Your mother," I said, but something didn't sound quite right.

"Yes." Grandpa took Grandma's hand in his.

"What do you mean when you say she appeared?"

"Just that," Grandpa said. "She seemingly came out of nowhere."

Just like the girl on the white horse.

"But she stayed. Married your father."

"That's right," he said. "Her name was Rebecca Becquerel."

I shook my head. I had a feeling that was supposed to mean something to me, but it didn't. He was trying to tell me something.

"That's right," he said. "But you see, Rebecca was from the future."

16

SYDNEY

I woke disoriented. Sunlight streamed in through the window across my face.

I was not at home in my condo and I was not at the hospital where I'd been known to spend the night a few times.

I was…

In Colorado.

In the ranch house.

I hadn't even realized I'd fallen asleep.

But something was different. No. Just about everything was different.

The fire had gone out. Not surprising.

But my blanket was gone, leaving me a bit chilly. I looked around. My handbag was not where I left it either.

Worried now, I sat up.

There was a basket of yarn where I had left my handbag. Yarn and knitting implements.

What the—?

The sofa had been moved back where I had found it.

There was a table on the wall to my left with fresh spring wildflowers.

My gaze was drawn back to the window. Two men rode past on horses.

Cowboys. At least they looked like cowboys. Anybody on a horse looked like a cowboy to me.

I didn't know whether to laugh or cry. Maybe both. At the same time.

Then I noticed the sounds of young people talking in the background.

The Auclair siblings.

No. That wasn't possible. That was in the 1800s.

This was the twenty-first century.

Not possible.

A slim young lady walked purposely to the fireplace and kneeling in front of it, began to brush the ashes into a pail.

"Hello," I said.

The girl jumped and turned around.

"I'm so sorry," I said. "I didn't mean to startle you."

"It's okay, Miss," she said.

The girl was wearing a long dress that looked like something someone in the 1800s would wear. The dress was a light brown, natural color and she wore a white apron over it.

It occurred to me, for no reason, that her apron wasn't going to be white very long with her cleaning out the sooty fireplace.

"I didn't know you were here," she said. "My apologies."

I had a decision to make in that moment. A decision that could determine how the rest of my day went and maybe even more.

No matter what decision I made, I would have to deal with it later, so since it didn't seem to matter so much either way, I went with the most logical decision.

I played along.

"I got here late," I said. "And didn't want to disturb anyone."

The girl looked confused as she looked over my jeans and denim jacket.

"Are you related to the Auclairs?" she asked tentatively.

"Yes," I said, going with my gut. I did, after all, have the same last name. "My name is Sydney Auclair."

"Oh," she said. "Miss Auclair. Of course. I will show you to the guest room."

"Okay," I said, a little impressed at her coping skills and feeling a little guilty. The girl had taken my word about who I was when I could be anyone.

And I was certain she had never heard of Sydney Auclair, but she showed no evidence of it.

I blew out a breath and started to follow her as she headed to the door.

But then she stopped and turned back around, her brow furrowed.

"I'll be right back," she said. "You can wait here while I make sure the room is ready."

Then she left me there in the sitting room as she should have.

She needed to confirm who I was.

17

___

ADAM

After a sleepless night, I got up early, before the sun was barely up at all, saddled Traveler, and took him on a run across the west pasture. Not to look at fences this time. Just to ride. To think.

Unfortunately, as I returned to the house, my thoughts were just as befuddled as they had been when I had set out.

My grandfather and grandmother, of whom I considered to be completely sane and grounded people had sat right there on the sofa in Grandma's sitting room and told me, right to my face, that my aunt had come from the future.

Not only that, but Uncle Jack had no more than laid his eyes on her—Rebecca Becquerel—than he had fallen head over heels in love.

It sounded so familiar that it had me reeling.

Like my uncle, I had no more than set eyes on… the girl on the white horse… whose name I did not know, when I had fallen head over heels. Just like that. Like she was some kind of siren.

Or that she had been sent here specifically for me. The thought made my gut clench with a swirl of fear and excitement. A woman sent all the way through time meant just for me. That was exciting in that she must be perfect for me and frightening that that could happen.

That's what Uncle Jack had gone to his grave believing. I had never known that, of course. I had never actually met my Uncle Jack. Something I regretted dearly. But there was nothing I could do about it. We had lived in West Virginia and Uncle Jack had traveled west when I was merely an infant. He'd come out here to Colorado and had been impressively successful with cattle and horse ranching.

Just building this house alone had been an accomplishment most men would never even undertake.

But the man had married a woman from the future.

As the house came into sight, the sun was up and the appetizing scent of bacon drifted from the house. Breakfast was a big meal around here. To take full advantage of the daily sunlight, we were all early risers. Animals had to be fed and chores had to be done.

I rode Traveler straight to the stables. My younger brothers would be out any moment to feed the horses. Then they would be confined to the classroom for most of the rest of the day. Sometimes I envied them with their excuse to stay inside and learn new things.

My sisters worked outside some. Everyone pitched in wherever they were needed.

After breakfast, I'd come back out. Do my chores. Put those two dapple grays back out in the pen together.

One of the horses need new shoes. Might do that today since the weather was nice.

I took some time brushing Traveler. I'd rode him pretty hard. Hadn't solved anything. I was right back where I started.

Pining after a mysterious girl who was quite very likely from the future.

Thinking back, she did have a different look to her.

Maybe it had been her hair, smooth and wavy. Maybe it had been her eyes.

When she'd looked into mine, it was as though she could see my very thoughts.

Whatever it was, she had me beguiled as my grandfather liked to say.

Maybe I'd look that word up in the dictionary one day. See exactly what it meant before I went around using it too much.

After Traveler was taken care of, I washed up and walked toward the house.

Before I reached the door, I came to a full stop.

She was standing right there in the window, looking out at me.

And this time, I was certain she saw me.

I slowly grinned and watched as the beginning of a little smile played about the corners of her lips.

It was enough for me.

I took off my hat, slapped it against my thigh, and hurried toward the door.

I was not going to let her slip away again this time.

At the very least, I needed to know her name. I needed to call her something in my head other than *girl.*

I went straight inside to the sitting room, ignoring the sounds of my family drifting from the kitchen. Breakfast would wait.

Or better, I'd take her to breakfast with me.

I reached the sitting room door and stopped.

She had turned and sunlight spilled through the window behind her, giving her an ethereal glow.

I swallowed hard.

"I don't know your name," I said.

18

SYDNEY

As I stood in the sitting room waiting for who I assumed was a young house maid to come back for me, I watched a horse and rider approaching.

Before they even passed by the window, I knew it was Adam. There was something about him that I recognized. The way he moved, even on a horse. The way he carried himself.

He was tall and handsome. Had that whole slightly disheveled cowboy look about him. He looked like maybe he hadn't shaved in a day or so and his hair was only a tiny bit longer than it would need to be for a professional cut, but I could see him in a business suit.

He could easily charm any girl with those handsome good looks.

Fortunately, I wasn't so easily charmed.

I waited until he came out of the barn.

He stopped when he saw me watching him.

And then he smiled at me.

Any resolve I thought I had at not being charmed by this man vanished in a heartbeat.

I put a hand against the window frame to steady myself.

Not only was I halfway charmed by this old ranch house deep in the heart of the Rocky Mountains, but I was completely charmed by Adam Auclair.

As he hurried inside, I took the moment to get myself together.

Just because I had seen the name Adam Auclair in what looked like a family Bible... with my name written next to it, did not mean that he was the same Adam Auclair or that I was the same Sydney Brandt.

The coincidence was too much to ignore. But it had been late at night and dark. I needed to look again in the light of day. To make sure that I had actually seen what I thought I saw.

There had to be a logical explanation.

Within seconds, he was standing at the door to the sitting room.

"I don't know your name," he said, without preamble.

"Sydney Brandt," I said, watching him carefully for any reaction, but he showed none. Clearly, he did not recognize my name.

I couldn't decide if I was relieved or disappointed.

Probably both. More disappointed than I wanted to admit, but I'd think about that later.

He walked up and took my hand in his. Held my fingers lightly in his hand.

"It's a pleasure to meet you Sydney Brandt," he said.

I nodded, not saying anything.

"Are you hungry?" he asked.

"Terribly." I ran a hand along my stomach. The scent of bacon and coffee was wreaking havoc on my stomach.

"I can get you some breakfast. Bring it to you. Or you can come with me and risk having to explain yourself to my family."

I was going to have to meet his family sooner or later since

I was apparently in their house. I had given up any illusion otherwise.

I had made the commitment to just go with it as long as it went, so go with it I would. Whatever *it* may turn out to be.

"Which do you recommend?" I asked.

He grinned. "Come on," he said. "Let's go to breakfast."

I followed him from the sitting room, through the larger parlor, toward the kitchen.

Everything looked so different. It was the same house, but instead of being dusty and old, it was clean and relatively newer. Not new, but newer.

The grandfather clock stood in the foyer, ticking away the minutes just as it had last night.

If this was my imagination, I was impressed by the vividness of the things I was able to create in my mind. Maybe I should start writing fiction.

Most people who had hallucinatory episodes described them in vague, hazy terms, but I was seeing everything sparkling clear with minute details.

Like the painting over the large stone fireplace. It was a hand painted scene of five young adult children, all in various poses at the edge of a mountain stream. Perhaps the same stream that I had crossed with my horse just yesterday. All wearing formal old-fashioned clothing. The girls in long hooped dresses. Three boys and two girls. The oldest boy was easily recognizable. It was Adam.

I glanced ahead at the live version of Adam. He grinned at me over his shoulder and my heart skipped a beat.

Nervous. I was nervous about meeting his family.

Wiping my trembling palms against my jeans, I considered this. I wasn't a nervous sort of person. I was a well-trained professional in my field. I treated patients who had everything from schizophrenia to depression to anxiety.

As I followed Adam down the hallway leading to the

kitchen where his family was gathered for breakfast, I concluded that this was not actually the kind of anxiety that I would treat. This was actually an excited kind of nervousness. The kind of excitement that a girl would feel on her first date or when she was getting engaged.

It was funny. During the time I had dated and even when I had gotten engaged to my ex- fiancé, I hadn't felt this kind of excited nervousness.

The last I could remember feeling this way was my senior year in high school. I'd been working the concession stand at one of the home games—homecoming in fact. The game was over and I was getting ready to leave when the quarterback of our high school team had stopped to get a coke.

I remembered every detail of the conversation.

"Sydney," David said. "What are you doing here?"

"Working." I pushed at my hair while I filled a paper cup with ice. Added coke. I was tired and doubtless had looked better. I'd licked off all my lipstick hours ago.

"I see," he said, taking a long drink through the straw. "Come to the dance with me."

"What dance?" I asked, knowing full well that there was only one dance he could possibly be talking about. The one everyone was going to tonight. The homecoming dance.

I remembered looking at him as though he must have lost any and all of his good sense. "Did someone sack you in the head?"

He laughed. "Hardly. We won."

"Don't you have a girlfriend? Edwina?" I knew he did. Everyone knew. They were an item.

What no one knew, however, was that I'd been crushing on David since junior high.

"Not anymore," he said. "We broke up."

"Just like that?"

"Nah. Can I get a refill?"

"I don't understand," I said as I refilled his coke.

"We've just been pretending to be together until after tonight's game."

"Why?" I handed him the cup.

"Why does anyone do anything?" Then he smiled at me and my world shifted out from under me.

"I can't," I'd told him. "I'm not dressed."

"No worries," he said. "I have to go home. Get cleaned up and change too. I'll pick you up in an hour."

Then he'd winked at me and walked away.

It hadn't worked out of course. After we'd gone to that homecoming dance, I had discovered that he and I had just about nothing in common and nothing at all to talk about.

But I'd never forgotten that little thrill that went all the way to my toes, leaving me almost too breathless to talk. That was the kind of nervousness I felt now. I hadn't felt it since then and hadn't expected to ever feel it again. I thought that kind of magic was a once in a life time thing and I had wasted mine on the fantasy of going out with the high school quarterback.

But here it was. In a world that couldn't be. With a man who didn't really exist.

The little thrill that went all the down to my toes and left my mind practically blank.

19

ADAM

Sydney Brandt.

That was the name of the girl I was going to marry.

She didn't know it, of course. No one knew it, much less her.

She would probably run from here as fast as she could.

I stopped, in the hallway, before we reached the kitchen, and looked at her.

"Where is your horse?" I asked, looking over her shoulder as though the horse would suddenly appear out the window behind her.

"My hor—" She shook her head, her brow furrowed in confusion.

"Your white horse," I said. "The one you rode in on."

"In the barn," she said with a little shrug.

I shook my head. "I just came from the barn. There was no white horse."

"Reggie," she said. "His name is Reggie."

"Your horse?"

"Yes."

"Reggie was not in the barn."

"Oh," she said, but I knew she didn't have an explanation. "I don't know then."

"Should we go look for him?"

"I don't think so." She bit her bottom lip and watched me, her gaze on mine. I could see that she was trying to figure out a good explanation, but I also knew that she didn't have one.

"It's okay," I said. "We'll find him after breakfast."

"Good idea," she said. "I'm sure we'll find him."

I wasn't so sure. But I didn't know how this time travel worked. And the more I spoke to her, I would bet money that she hadn't even figured out that she was from the future.

By the time we got into the breakfast room, my siblings had left for their classroom and my grandfather had gone off with Mr. Evette to fish in the stream again.

The only person left in the room was Grandma. She was straightening up plates and glasses my siblings had left strewn about the table.

"Good morning, Grandma," I said, taking Sydney's hand and pulling her forward to stand next to me. "This is Sydney Brandt."

Grandma's eyes widened and she looked at me questioningly.

"Is this… the girl you saw yesterday?"

"Yes."

Grandma looked to Sydney. "Please excuse my sudden lack of manners. I blame it on trying to keep up with five young people and a husband."

Sydney stepped forward and took Grandma's hands in hers.

"No need to apologize," she said. "I completely understand. And I apologize for intruding on you this way. Please. Let me help you."

"Nonsense," Grandma said. "Sit. I'll have Frederick scramble some fresh eggs for you two to have a hot meal."

"That's not nec—"

"Sit," Grandma said. "It might not seem like it, but we brought our southern hospitality out west with us."

Sydney glanced at me, then sat down as instructed. I sat down in the chair beside her.

Grandma headed off toward the kitchen.

"I hope you're hungry," I said. "You're about to have a huge breakfast."

"I don't mind," she said, smiling at me.

My heart did some unnatural flips. I sat back and decided I might as well get used to that. A man fortunate enough to have the perfect woman land in the middle of his parlor had to get used to having his heart flutter in an unnatural fashion now and then.

20

SYDNEY

I glanced out the window. I'd tried to seem unconcerned about Reggie, the beautiful white horse I had ridden in on, but truly I was concerned. I had left the horse outside in the rain all night. It wasn't raining now, but when I'd fallen asleep, as far as I knew, he was still out there. He could have gotten loose. Mr. White would be very upset, rightly so, if his horse was lost, injured, or stolen. And I would feel terrible about it. He had trusted me, a stranger to him, with the horse.

"You didn't see Reggie?" I asked, having second thoughts about not going out to look for the horse.

Adam shook his head. "No sign of him."

Either Reggie had gotten away in the night, he was injured, or… there was one other possibility that I couldn't allow my thoughts to visit. Whenever I got near it, it was like my thoughts slammed against a brick wall and bounced off.

"Maybe you're right," I said. "Maybe we should look for him."

"Maybe," Adam said. He was looking at me funny now. It

seemed he, too, was having second thoughts about the possibility of finding the horse.

"Here you go," Mrs. Auclair said, bringing in two plates heaped with eggs and bacon and toast.

"This is too much," I said. "You shouldn't have gone to this much trouble."

"It was no trouble," she said.

Even as I protested, I picked up a fork and began eating. I truly was starved.

I'd cleaned over half my plate when I realized they were both watching me.

"How long has it been since you ate, Dear?" Mrs. Auclair asked.

"I'm not sure," I said, trying to think back. "I didn't have anything yesterday. Except... a coffee. So it was the night before that."

I shrugged. I'd had times in graduate school that I had forgotten to eat. I had a strange metabolism that allowed me not be hungry and to go without thinking about food for long periods of time.

"Well, you're here now," she said. "You won't go hungry again."

"Thank you," I said. "You're very kind." I looked over at Adam. "Both of you."

Mrs. Auclair clasped her hands in front of her. "Eat," she said. "Don't let us stop you."

"It was wonderful," I said, straightening in my chair and feeling a bit embarrassed that I had eaten so much before they even started eating.

I hid my embarrassment behind my juice glass. The orange juice was wonderfully fresh.

"Is this fresh-squeezed?" I asked.

Mrs. Auclair looked at me funny again. "Of course."

I picked up a piece of toast and nibbled on it while Adam ate.

Mrs. Auclair leaned toward me. "Tell us where you're from."

"Boston," I said.

"You had a long trip getting here."

"A little," I said. "I've never been this far west."

Adam and his grandmother glanced at each other.

I set down the toast and wiped my hands on my white cloth napkin.

Adam pushed his plate away. "Grandma," he said. "We're going outside. See if we can find her horse."

"That's a good idea," she said. "I think I'll go to my sitting room and do some knitting."

"Do you want me to help clean this up?" I asked.

"No need. Frederick will get it," Adam said, taking my hand and leading out the back door.

I got the distinct feeling that he wanted to get me away from his grandmother.

Maybe he was just rescuing me from her questions.

Maybe he knew she would ask questions I couldn't answer.

21

ADAM

It was a beautiful day. The sun was shining brightly, but white clouds hung low over the steep Rocky Mountains. It was going to snow. It didn't matter that it was Spring. I'd seen snow in July up here in the mountains.

We needed to make a run into Whiskey Springs for supplies, but we would wait until the threat of snow had passed. Besides, the river was swollen with snow-melt.

Not the best time for traveling with a wagon. Horses would do okay, but a wagon could get bogged down.

I needed to get Sydney away from my grandmother. Grandma was biting her tongue. Trying to act like nothing was awry, but I could see her struggling not to just jump in there and start asking Sydney questions. Her good breeding was the only thing stopping her. It would be rude to ask too many personal questions of a stranger, especially one staying in your house. And like Grandma had said, she had brought her good manners with her from West Virginia here to Colorado.

There would be plenty of time for her to talk to Sydney later. If I had anything to do with it, Sydney wasn't going anywhere.

We walked around to the front of the house first and stopped at the hitching post.

"I left him right here," Sydney said. "It was raining."

"Raining? You left him in the rain?"

Her brow furrowed with consternation, she looked up at me. "I thought… I didn't…"

"It's okay," I said. "We keep our horses in the barn, but it doesn't hurt them to stay out in the weather."

"What if he broke loose?" she asked. "Will he come back?"

Now, like Grandma, I was biting my tongue. I didn't think Reggie was here. I would put money on Reggie being in the future where she had left him.

But I didn't want to frighten her by telling her this.

Grandpa had suggested that I let her figure out for herself that she was from the future.

And besides, there was the possibility that I was wrong. Sydney may have just wandered away from her family. She could simply be lost. I decided to explore that a bit.

"Who did you travel with?" I asked. "From Boston?"

"I traveled alone," she said, obviously thinking nothing of it. She had one hand shading her eyes, searching from here to the horizon for her horse.

Even if Reggie was out there, it would be highly unlikely that she would be able to see him from here. Being a white horse, he would blend in with the environment.

"Right." I took off my hat and ran a hand over my hair. "Did you come by train or wagon?"

She smiled and shifted her gaze to mine. "Airplane," she said.

Focusing on her sparkling green eyes that reminded me of an alpine meadow in spring, just after the snowmelt, her answer just slid right past me.

·　·　·

"WE'RE NOT GOING to find him, are we?" she asked.

I swallowed thickly and tried to focus on what she was saying.

I shook my head. "Do you think we will?"

"A question with a question," she said, with a delicate lift of her right eyebrow. "An exceptionally effective way to avoid answering."

"Well," I said. "I don't know about that, but, no, I don't think we're going to find your horse."

She nodded and looked away.

22

SYDNEY

The alpine wind whipped at my hair. Since I didn't have a hair band with me, I gathered it up and held it off my face with my hand.

It was so beautiful here. We were in a valley, high in the mountains. The rugged peaks of the Rocky Mountains looked almost close enough to touch. They weren't, of course. They were probably miles away.

I shook my head at myself when I realized I was searching for mountain climbers on the rugged ledges. I had a very distinct feeling that there were no mountain climbers. I didn't know exactly when people started climbing for sport, but I was pretty sure it was not now.

I was slowly coming to the conclusion that I was not in my own time.

It wasn't just seeing the family tree with my name in it.

It was the little things.

Adam had asked me if I'd come by train or wagon. When I said I'd come by airplane, my answer had seemed to go right past him.

If I was right and I was in the 1870s, then the word airplane would mean absolutely nothing to him.

The house was probably the biggest indication of this being some point in the past… other than Adam and his family, of course.

It was possible they were just people who lived off the grid. With no television and no modern conveniences. But it was clear to me that in that case they would have been here last night. I was clearly the one out of place.

If I was wrong, I'd deal with it later, but there was something to be said for being able to adapt to one's surroundings and I felt like I was pretty good at that.

I could put myself aside and into the world of a patient. It was one of the things that made me good at what I did.

My patients *felt* understood because I was able to connect with them wherever they were.

Maybe that was what I was doing with Adam. Maybe I had somehow fallen into his brain and was seeing the world from his viewpoint.

Either that or I had traveled back in time.

"Can we walk down to the river?" I asked.

"Of course."

He took my hand and tucked it into the crook of his elbow as we walked.

It was a very gentlemanly gesture. Very old-fashioned.

"What is it you do here?" I asked.

"What do you mean?" he asked.

"Being from back east, I don't know much about ranching." That, at least, was most definitely the truth. "I was just wondering if you could explain it to me." I nearly found myself batting my eyelashes, but caught myself.

"Okay." He looked around as though trying to figure out where to start. "Besides cattle, we raise horses." He pointed to a couple of gorgeous dapple grays in a pen to our right.

"We've put those two together hoping they'll breed. So far they don't seem particularly taken with each other."

"Maybe they're too much alike," I said.

"How so?"

"Well they look alike, so they might think they're related."

Adam rubbed his chin. "Maybe."

So they didn't use artificial insemination. Another point on the time travel side of my mental ledger.

As we continued our walk along the path that had been a dirt road yesterday, I realized that the only one of my mental columns that had anything at all in it was the time travel one.

23

ADAM

S ydney clearly knew nothing about ranching.

I could tell by her comments and the questions she asked. So much so that I was surprised she even knew how to ride a horse.

But she could learn. Everyone had to start somewhere.

And she seemed interested and curious.

Those were points in her favor. Not that she needed them.

If she'd asked me to move away from here… to go live with her in Boston… at the moment, at least, I was pretty sure I'd be packing my things.

But fortunately she seemed interested in the ranch.

"Where are all the cows?" she asked.

"They're in the lower pasture," I said.

"Where?"

I pointed in the general direction off to my left. "A few miles that way. With ten thousand acres, you can't even begin to see all our property from here."

She stopped and turned to face me, searching my eyes.

"How many acres?

"Ten thousand."

"Yes," she said, walking again. "That's what I thought you said."

"It's one of the biggest ranches south of Montana."

"Yes, I suppose it is," she said with a little smile.

I wish I knew what she was thinking. If she really was from the future, then she would know things.

"You seem surprised that we have that many acres," I said.

She nodded. "It's impressive."

So she wasn't going to tell me if she did know anything. At least not yet.

Reaching the river, we stood on a boulder at the edge of the bank and looked down at the water swirling over the rocks.

"The river is flooded," she said.

I nodded. "The snowmelt."

"Uh huh."

"You already knew that," I said, looking over at her.

"It was like this yesterday," she said. "When I came in."

"I see." *Was that before or after you went back in time?*

She smiled over at me.

"Look," I said. "There's a fish. Swimming upstream. You don't have that in Boston, I bet."

"Nah," she said. "But I saw one yesterday."

"Right." I wasn't sure just how much longer I was going to be able to keep myself from coming right out and talking to her about the time travel. I wanted desperately to know if she knew. Somehow it seemed overwhelmingly important that I find out if she knew she was... possibly was... from the future.

"What else did you see yesterday?"

She turned and, raising her face to the sun, closed her eyes.

I decided she wasn't going to answer me.

"I couldn't begin to tell you," she said.

24

SYDNEY

I wanted to tell Adam that I believed I was from the future. I really wanted to tell him. To find out what year it was, at the very least.

But I didn't want him to think I was insane.

I laughed out loud.

"What's funny?" he asked.

"Nothing," I said. But it was funny that I was worried he would think I was insane.

I treated insanity every day. Granted, insanity was the legal definition of mental illness, but there was nothing I could do about popular vernacular and I certainly wasn't going to try.

It wasn't just that, but I just might actually be a bit... a lot... insane at the moment.

Just go with it.

I turned and faced him.

"Have you ever heard my name before today?" I asked.

He shook his head. "No."

"Have you ever met anyone named Sydney?"

"I can truthfully say that I have not."

So the name I'd seen written in their family Bible... my

name… and the year 1879 could only be mine. What were the odds that another Sydney Brandt was going to show up at his door and marry him.

Unless…

"What year is it?" I blurted.

"1879."

He said it without hesitation.

"Well then," I said.

"Well then what?"

"Nothing," I said again. *If we were going to get married in 1879, we didn't have much time left.*

"Didn't sound like nothing," he said.

I shrugged and adjusted the hand that was still tucked in the crook of his elbow. I could get used to this.

Maybe it was because we were standing on the edge of a rushing river, but my arm linked with his made me feel decidedly safe.

I'd made my decision to go with where I found myself.

And apparently I had found myself in 1879.

What that meant I couldn't say. Perhaps it was only temporary.

The thought should have left me with a feeling of relief, knowing that this was probably temporary, but instead it settled in my stomach like a rock.

I didn't want it to be temporary.

I shifted from one foot to the other and looked at Adam out of the corner of my eyes.

It was his fault, I decided. It was his fault for having such fascinating blue eyes that looked at me as though I was the only woman he had ever so much as looked at.

Of course, living out here, it was possible. Not likely, but possible.

And that wouldn't be such a bad thing. In my world, there were too many people. Sometimes I thought that having too many choices was a bad thing. Especially for a maximizer. I suppose I was a maximizer. More like an avoider, really, when it came to men.

But with so many ways to meet people and so many people to meet, it was no wonder that people in modern society had trouble with relationships.

I smiled over at him.

"Sorry," I said. "I was just thinking."

"You seem to do a lot of that."

"That's a very good observation."

He shrugged. "I tend to do some thinking myself at times."

25

ADAM

I liked Sydney's laugh—like an angel. I liked her eyes —sparkling green intelligent and seductive... and mysterious. I liked her hair—long, silky, tousled, the color of a storm hanging low in the sky.

I liked everything about her.

It didn't matter that I had already decided I wanted to marry her. People got married for a lot of reasons.

I could marry her simply because she and I would make beautiful children. That was a perfectly valid reason in and of itself.

And, of course, there was the thing about the time travel— about her practically falling into my lap.

But it wasn't that either. Not only that, anyway.

The more time I spent with her, the more I liked her.

The more I wanted to know about her.

"Tell me about Boston," I said. "About your life there."

"I work in a hospital," she said.

"You don't say. You're a nurse?"

"No," she said with a little smile, looking away from me.

"What then?"

"I 'um. I talk to people. To try to make them feel better."

"Oh. I see. A volunteer." I watched as a fish swam upstream, but didn't bother to point it out to her.

"Something like that," she said.

"Do you write letters, too?" I caught my breath. There was something I never talked about, but I suddenly felt compelled to tell her. "A volunteer wrote my father's last letter. In the war. Before he…" I faltered. I couldn't say the words out loud. It was too painful.

"It's okay," she said, putting her other hand on mine. "You don't have to say anything. I don't like to see you hurting."

How had she known I was hurting? "Thank you."

"Can we sit down?" she asked.

"Of course." I led her away from the river to a log where I often sat when I needed to think.

The first thing I was going to do as soon as we made our first trip into Whiskey Springs was to buy her some proper clothes. I'd buy her a pretty gown. Green to match her eyes.

"Why did you come west?" I asked.

"My uncle," she said. "Uncle Jack… asked me to come. I didn't know…"

"You got a letter from him?" I asked. I was still confused about how Uncle Jack had contacted her. He'd been gone before she was even born.

It had something to do with the time travel.

"Something like that," she said again.

"Uncle Jack has been gone since before you were born," I said.

"I know." She put a hand on my arm. Then looked up and met my gaze. "I know. I don't understand it either."

"How do you make sense of it?" I asked. "All this?"

She shook her head. "I don't. But…" She paused and looked at me as though choosing her words carefully. Her kissable lips were slightly parted.

"What is it?" I asked, taking both her hands in mine.
"I have a rather odd request."
"Okay," I said. "Just tell me what it is and I'll do it."
Whatever it was, I would give it my best.
I was enchanted.

26

———

SYDNEY

*B*y the time we got back to the house, everything was in an uproar.

The steady rush of the river had blocked any sounds that might have alerted us to trouble.

"Something's not right," Adam said as we neared the back door.

The fact that he knew the house much better than I did confirmed my own suspicions.

"I agree," I said.

When he shot me a sideways glance, I just shrugged. I guess he had hoped I would disagree.

We walked past the empty schoolroom, books strewn everywhere, but no students.

Voices drifted from the direction of the parlor.

The grandfather clock began to chime the hour as we walked past.

Everyone had gathered in the sitting room where I had spent the night.

Adam increased his stride, leaving me to catch up.

"What's happened?" he asked, alarm evident in his voice.

Mrs. Auclair looked up. I saw fear in her eyes. Fear and panic. But she held herself still. When she went to wring out the cloth she held, her hands trembled visibly.

"It's your grandfather," she said. "He fell in the river."

Adam rushed to his grandfather's side. Mr. Auclair lay on the couch, one foot hanging over the end, a blanket over him. His other foot was propped on an ottoman shoved up against the couch. He looked exceptionally uncomfortable.

The fire in the fireplace was making the room almost unbearably warm.

"What happened?" Adam asked. "Are you hurt?"

"He fell," another man standing nearby answered. "We think his leg is broken and he may have bumped his head."

"Did someone go for the doctor?" Adam asked.

"Of course," Mrs. Auclair said.

Adam pulled over a wooden chair so he could sit next to his grandfather. "Is he sleeping?" he asked.

"I'm not asleep," Grandpa said. "They plied me with whiskey."

Adam looked up at his Grandma.

"He's sleeping," she said.

"Dozing," Grandpa corrected, not bothering to open his eyes.

"How did you get him back here with a broken leg?" he asked to no one in particular.

"It was no small endeavor," the man said.

The room was packed. Besides Mr. and Mrs. Auclair, there was the man—the fishing partner, and the woman who must be the children's tutor.

And there were the children. They weren't really children. The youngest was no younger than thirteen. So all teenagers.

Feeling intrusive, I backed out of the room.

I had been so stunned to see my own name in the family

Bible that I hadn't taken the time to look at any of the other dates.

I didn't have, and was quite thankful that I didn't, any knowledge about how long anyone lived.

I had asked Adam to let me see his family's Bible and we had been on our way to do just that when we discovered that his grandfather had been injured.

I wandered away from the sitting room, away from this family, obviously in a state of crisis. There was nothing I could do to help them.

I had a little bit of medical training, but setting a broken leg was way beyond anything I was qualified to do.

They said maybe he bumped his head. I could do an assessment there, even though I didn't know his baseline.

I wouldn't be able to make a definite diagnosis, but no one was requiring me to do that.

This was 1879. No one had any expectations at all.

While I waited, I stopped in front of the grandfather clock and watched the steady movement of the pendulum. The clock was so tall, I had to look up to see the time, at least standing this close to it. From a distance, it was a lot easier to see the time.

When the clock began to chime the hour, I jumped, startled. The chime echoed through the house.

The fire here, in the parlor, burned low, seemingly forgotten. I went over, picked up a heavy iron poker and shifted the logs so that the flames burned brightly again.

I wandered to the front window. Put my hand on the thick, smooth velvet drapes that framed the view and looked out. There was a storm brewing in the distance. A nasty looking storm that was headed this way. The clouds were dark, pierced by streaks of lightning.

The wind had picked up, too, blowing leaves and other

debris around the yard. I found it odd that there was so much dust in the air.

A movement outside the window, off to my right caught my attention.

It was Reggie.

I blinked, not believing what I was seeing, but the horse was standing right there. Someone must have found him and brought him back. Tied him back where I had left him.

I was so pleased to see the horse. Reggie was my link to sanity. To the world as I knew it.

While the family was dealing with Grandpa, I would go out. Maybe lead Reggie to the barn. Feed him, at least.

My hand on the cool wood of the window frame, I turned around and had to clutch the window pane to keep from losing my balance.

The two sofas in the parlor were covered with white sheets.

The fireplace was cold and looked like it hadn't been used for ages.

The grandfather clock was… just gone.

And the house was silent.

27

ADAM

We managed to get Grandpa upstairs to his bedroom. Grandpa was not a small man by any means. It took me, Mr. Evette, and Paul.

He insisted that he was going to be okay. He had a headache, but that was to be expected.

Mr. Evette seemed to think that Grandpa's leg was broken, but I wasn't convinced. Not completely. It didn't look broken to me. Bruised perhaps. But Grandpa being elderly, it may as well be broken. It would take him a long time to heal. Either way, when the doctor got here, we would know for sure.

Grandma sat next to him, keeping a cool cloth on his forehead. She was quiet. Quieter than I had ever seen her.

I sent my siblings outside to do chores. I figured they were too worried to concentrate on the books, but some physical labor would do them good.

Mr. Evette returned to the stream where Grandpa had fallen to get the things they had left behind.

It wasn't long before Grandpa was definitely sleeping. Snoring, in fact.

"Will you be okay, Grandma?" I asked. "For a few minutes? I need to find Sydney."

"Of course," she said, barely noticing me as she adjusted the blankets around her husband. The two of them had been married since they were no more than teenagers. I didn't know what one would do without the other. That was something it didn't pay to even begin to think about.

Grandpa would be okay. He was a fiercely strong man. He'd made the trip from West Virginia to Colorado twice and one time back. Once with a wife and once with five grandchildren. From where I was sitting, he could do anything.

The house had a somber feel to it as I made my way downstairs. It was as though everyone was waiting. Perhaps waiting on Doc Avery to get here. Or maybe just waiting for Grandpa to be up and about.

I'd never known him to even be so much as sick a day in his life.

This was very unsettling.

Perhaps Sydney could help with that. It was her job at the hospital to listen to people. She would understand.

I didn't see her downstairs. Frederick hadn't seen her. I stood in the middle of the parlor and considered where she might have gone.

The barn. Maybe she had gone outside to look for her horse.

As I stepped outside, I realized that there was a storm coming. Not a snow storm as I had predicted, but a thunderstorm.

I put a hand over my eyes and looked down the road that led to the river. The road that led to Whiskey Springs.

That's when I saw her. It was far in the distance, almost too far to see in the blowing dust, but it was Sydney I saw on her white horse.

It was just for a moment. When I blinked, they were gone.

A trick of the light.

The storm was making things look different.

Sometimes a man saw what he was looking for. If he looked hard enough.

It had only been my imagination.

At least that's what I told myself.

But I knew better.

I knew that Sydney had gone back to her time.

28

SYDNEY

I found my handbag in the sitting room next to the sofa right where I had left it.

I grabbed it up and headed outside, practically running.

"Hey Reggie," I said, rubbing his nose for a second. "I'm so sorry I left you standing here like this."

Then I stuck my foot in the stirrup and pulled myself up onto the horse's back.

Outrunning the storm, leaving it behind us, Reggie and I followed the road that led to the river. I knew where to cross now. I knew how to get back to my car. All I had to do was follow the riverbank a ways down and cross there in that wide shallow part where the water was actually friendly and tame.

But it was getting dark. The storm was on my heels.

The wind whipped at my hair, leaving it tangled and tousled. I didn't care.

But when I reached the riverbank, before turning left toward the crossing place, I stopped. This was the exact spot where I had stood just an hour, at most, with Adam.

The rocks had not changed. The water was the same. Deep and swirling. Fish swimming upstream in the cold water.

Everything was the same.

But I was different.

Looking up, I saw a jet passing high overhead, leaving a white stream behind it.

I was home.

But I had spent the day in the past. With Adam.

Somehow. Someway.

And it had been wonderful.

I had never been out west until Uncle Jack had left me this ranch… what was left of it, anyway.

Back in 1879, the house was sitting on ten thousand acres owned by the Auclairs. Now there was only fifteen hundred left. It was still a lot of land, but not nearly as much as they had started with.

Yet it was still wilderness. The area around the house was still uncommercialized.

I wondered if Mr. White lived on part of the land that had been the Auclair's. Maybe if I had a map.

I wondered what had caused them to sell.

What if…

A clear image of Adam's face came to mind. His sparkling blue eyes that smiled at me like I was the only girl he had ever been interested in.

Like I was everything.

No one had ever looked at me like that.

Not the high school quarterback and not even my ex-fiancé.

Reggie shook his head when a flash of lightning was followed almost immediately by a crash of thunder.

If I didn't move now, I was going to be caught in the storm. Probably not the safest thing to have happen.

As the wind whipped around me, sweeping hair into my eyes, I sat immobilized on the back of the beautiful white horse.

What if Grandpa Auclair's accident had led to the sale of a huge chunk of the land?

What if I had been sent here so I could help the Auclair family?

Could I live with myself if I simply abandoned them like this?

So many questions I didn't have the answers to.

Reggie's ears twitched. He was getting nervous as the storm powered over us. Rightly so. We were going to be caught in the middle of it.

But I was frozen in place.

What if I never saw Adam again?

29

ADAM

I saddled my horse and took off toward the river at a gallop. Riding right into the storm.

Traveler was a good horse. He didn't so much as blink in protest.

Somewhere in the back of my mind, I knew I wasn't being rational.

If Sydney had her horse, Reggie, then she was back in the future.

There was no way I was going to be able to get to her.

But if there was any chance… any chance at all… I had to take it.

Even if I couldn't convince her to stay, perhaps I could see her one more time.

Just one more time.

I felt compelled to tell her how I felt.

I wanted her to know before she returned to Boston.

The wind whipped at my white shirt. I should have worn a jacket. But there had been no time to think.

I nudged Traveler to run faster.

The storm swirled around us now.

Lightning flashed and thunder crashed.

I had gone insane.

I pulled on the horse's reins, bringing him to a stop, muttered something to myself. Something I couldn't repeat in polite company.

It was time to go back. I had responsibilities. Things to do. It would do no one any good for me to be struck by lightning out here.

In between the flashes of lightning, I heard the steady rush of the river up ahead.

I was about to turn around, berating myself for not having a lick of good sense when I saw her.

Sitting there at the edge of the riverbank on the back of her white horse, facing me.

Sydney.

Her hair flowing around her, she watched me.

Lightning flashed and thunder crashed around us. The storm was full upon us. Raindrops pierced my skin and soaked my shirt.

I was frozen in place.

Sydney lifted her arm, stretched it out toward me.

I lifted my arm, too. Held it out in her direction.

I could barely see her in the curtain of rain.

A bolt of lightning flashed over her, lighting the air around her, giving her an ethereal glow. The glow was all around her. Otherworldly.

I held my breath. This was too much to bear.

Every nerve in my body. Every cell screamed at me to go to her, but I couldn't get my body to cooperate.

I gust of wind blew rain into my eyes and I blinked.

When I opened my eyes, she was gone.

And she had taken my heart with her.

30

———————

SYDNEY

I was a logical, rational person. I made good decisions and I helped other people make good decisions.

When people made bad decisions, they often ended up in the hospital and that was when I could help them.

After stashing Reggie in the barn, tossing what little hay I could find into his stall, I walked to the house, the rain swirling around me. I was soaked.

But I dragged my hopefully waterproof hard case suitcase along behind me. At least I had a change of clothes now.

I had to admit that this was one of the most nonsensible things I had ever done.

Well, I told myself as I squared my shoulders and pulled the key to the house out of my pocket. I was overdue for a little nonsensibleness.

I'd made a dash to my car and after strapping my suitcase onto the back of the horse, I'd ridden back across the river to the ranch in the rain.

Adam had come after me.

I had dashed and run out of the house when I'd seen Reggie outside. It had been some kind of panicky reflex.

But when I'd taken the time to think about it. And when I had seen Adam holding out his arm toward me, I had realized that running away from him was not what I wanted to do.

I could not in good conscience leave here, with things like they were, and return to my life in Boston.

It was everything. It was Grandpa Auclair who had fallen in the river. He might need me. I could help him and his family deal with an injury like that.

Brain damage was not my specialty by any stretch. My specialty was psychosis. I knew how to treat schizophrenia, depression, and anxiety.

Ha. Maybe I needed to treat myself for psychosis.

After getting inside the house and locking the door, the first thing I did was to build a fire in the sitting room. My little stash of firewood wasn't going to last very long, but I didn't expect it to have to.

Then I changed clothes. I put on a floral cotton nightgown that I'd had forever. It was the only sleepwear I had brought with me. I put on my UGGs house slippers. They were really UGGs booties, but I wore them for house slippers.

Dressed for bed, I snuggled beneath the blankets I'd left on the sofa in the sitting room and stared into the flames.

I needed to think.

In the morning, when it was light, I would explore the house as I should have already done. I needed to study the family Bible. If it was still there. And maybe there were other things stashed away that would give me some clue as to the fate of the Auclairs.

I hadn't met Adam's brothers and sisters, but I'd met his grandmother. I felt like I knew her.

Nonetheless, it was Adam that I was here for. Without Adam, this would simply be one of those mysteries in life that I would tell my grandchildren.

Maybe I would just write a story about it. It would make a good children's fairytale. I'd put a happy ending on it, of course. Adam and I would live together happily ever after.

Entertaining myself with that possibility, I fell asleep.

31

ADAM

"Where have you been?" Paul asked as I walked in through the backdoor.

"Where does it look like I've been?" I scowled at my brother, feeling especially moody and out of sorts.

"Looks like you got caught in the rain," Paul said. He was sitting alone at the breakfast table having cheese and bread.

I grumbled something and headed upstairs to get out of my soaked clothes. I couldn't help but hear Paul's laughter behind me.

He could laugh all he wanted. I didn't care.

I'd just watched the woman who had my heart vanish. Again. Only this time, she wasn't just a mysterious girl. She was the one I wanted to marry.

I continued to grumble to myself as I made my way upstairs to my bedroom.

After I changed into clean clothes, I needed to check on my grandfather. To see if they had heard anything from Doc Alexander.

He probably wasn't coming tonight. Not in this storm. He would be crazy if he did.

Maybe he would fit right in, I admitted as I closed my door and began peeling off my clothes. After Sydney had vanished, I'd waited there in the rain for what must have been an hour.

But I'd known in my heart that she wasn't coming back. She had vanished through the portal or whatever it was that took her away from me back to her own time.

To the future.

I tossed my wet clothes aside in a pile and dried off with a towel.

It was selfish of me to want her to stay here. There was no way of knowing what she might be giving up by staying here in the past.

I couldn't even begin to imagine what it must be like in the future.

There would probably be more people. That was about as far as my brain could go with that one.

I wasn't ignorant. I'd done my share of reading and I took care of the family accounts, but I had always considered myself to be a practical man.

Responsible.

I had my family to take care of. Finding a wife had never been at the top of my priority list. It was one of those someday… maybe… if not, it could be okay… kind of things.

But now that I had met Sydney, my perspective on that had changed.

I didn't want just any wife. I wanted her.

I put on dry clothes, poured a whiskey for myself, and went outside through the French doors to stand on the balcony outside my room.

The rain had moved on. The storm was over.

But storm inside me still raged.

Rain drops fell from the leaves of the fir trees outside. An owl hooted out a greeting. I just stood silently.

There was more than a possibility that I would never see

Sydney again. She had been here in my life for a fleeting moment.

But I wasn't going anywhere. If she ever returned, I would be here for her.

Even if people called me insane. I didn't care. I was going to wait right here.

For the rest of my life if that's what it took.

32

SYDNEY

*S*omething woke me in the dead of night. Perhaps I had been dreaming. I actually thought I'd heard the chiming of the grandfather clock.

But when I opened my eyes, I knew it had been no more than a dream. The house was quiet. The only sound was the flicker of the flames in the fireplace and the wind howling around the outside of the house.

The house was high enough in elevation that there was always a wind blowing. This would not be good land for farming. Not that I knew a single thing about farming.

I lay perfectly still for a long time, listening for any unusual sounds in the night. An owl hooted outside in one of the spruce trees near the window. A wolf howled in the distance and a few minutes later another answered. Mournful and lonely.

I shuddered. But I was safe inside the house. I'd checked all the door and windows and the house was perfectly intact, if not worse for wear.

Everything considered, it must have been very well built to have lasted this long, especially being left unattended for so many years. Houses died when no one lived inside them. It was the strangest thing. It was like they needed humans to stay alive just as we needed them.

I wondered what Adam was doing right now. Asleep, of course. Since my phone had run down, I had no way of knowing what time it was.

I thought about getting up and poking at the fire. Maybe add some wood to it. But I didn't want to leave the warmth of my blankets.

I couldn't stay here for very long. I needed food.

The realtor had been supposed to meet me at the driveway yesterday. I'd forgotten all about that. What had she thought when she'd seen my car? Had she come looking for me?

Maybe I had been reported missing. I would have some explaining to do when I got back and returned the horse to Mr. White. I hoped that my car was still there.

It was supposed to be returned to the rental agency at the Denver airport... tomorrow... maybe the next day. I'd lost track of the days.

I dozed off again, lulled to sleep by the steady howling of the wind. I imagined I heard the stream roaring in the distance, but I couldn't be sure.

When I woke again, sunlight streamed across my face.

I was in my condo. The neighbors were cooking something again. I rarely cooked, but they cooked a lot and the scent often drifted to my condo, especially when I left a window cracked for fresh air. Smelled like they were frying bacon today.

The street outside was quiet. I listened very intently for the sound of cars traveling up and down the street. Maybe the street had been closed off for some kind of event. A marathon maybe. Runners came right by here.

No. That didn't seem right.

The steady ticking of the clock penetrated my awareness. The grandfather clock.

As I slowly opened my eyes, I became aware of other sounds. A roaster. There were no roasters where I lived.

Teenagers laughing and talking.

"Good morning."

My heart stopped, then did all sorts of flips and turns.

I blinked, but the sunlight blinded me.

Still. I knew that voice.

It was Adam.

I had gone back to the past.

I should have been upset. I should have been concerned.

But this was where I had set out to go when I had come back—in the storm, no less—to the house last night.

My lack of concern troubled me.

I bit my lip to keep from laughing out loud. I was worried about not being worried.

People who experienced a psychogenic fugue weren't concerned. In fact, when faced with the reality of who they were, they usually fought to maintain their new identity and not let go of their past.

I didn't have a new identity. Not exactly anyway.

I just had a new time.

This was most definitely not in the DSM.

It was a psychosis all my own.

And it was wrapped up and tied in the bow of time travel.

33

ADAM

I sat in the armchair and watched Sydney sleep. I hardly blinked at all for fear that she would vanish.

How many men watched their girl sleep? Hundreds. Thousands. But I would bet everything I had that not another one of them hardly dared to look away for fear that she would vanish back into her own time.

By the time I had finally fallen asleep last night, it was almost daybreak.

I'd lain awake, unable to turn off my brain. There were so many things I needed to figure out. So many possibilities.

When Grandma knocked on my door, I had jumped out of bed and pulled on my pants. I always slept in a long white short sleeved cotton shirt. No one ever came to my door in the night, or any time for that matter. As adult children, we at least had our privacy.

I opened the door with dread, thinking that Grandpa had taken a turn for the worst. He could have caught his death from falling into the freezing water.

Instead she had just looked at me with a strange expression.

"Sydney is sleeping in my sitting room," she said. "When she wakes up, you can show her to the guest room." She turned on her heel without saying anything else.

"Of course," I nodded, somehow keeping a straight face until the door closed between us.

Then I had been unable to keep from grinning from ear to ear. I quickly finished getting dressed and made my way downstairs.

Careful not to wake her, I sat in an armchair and watched her sleep until she woke on her own.

"Good morning," I said.

She struggled to sit up. "Good morning."

"We have the guest room ready for you."

"I don't want to intrude," she said.

I looked at her quizzically. "That's an odd thing to be concerned with at this point."

She smiled a little. "It is, isn't it?"

"It's okay," I said, pouring her a glass of water and handing it to her.

She drank all of it, then looked at me with those deep green eyes of hers.

"What do you think we're supposed to do now?" she asked.

"I have some ideas." I managed to keep a straight face.

"No," she said, but I saw the faint blush on her cheeks. "Seriously."

"Seriously, I don't have a clue." But now that she asked. "We need to talk to my grandfather."

"How is he?" she asked.

"I haven't heard."

"How could you not know with him being here in the same house?"

"It's a big house," I said with a shrug.

She nodded and gathered one of the blankets more closely around her shoulders. "I understand. I got a little lost upstairs."

"Are you cold?" I asked.

"A little," she said. "But the fire is warm. Thanks for feeding it."

"You should be able to wear one of my sister's dresses."

"She's so young," she said.

"You're quite thin," he pointed out.

"That's a good thing," she said.

I tilted my head to the side and looked at her. "The future must be an interesting place."

"You could say that. Things aren't like they are now."

"I can't even begin to imagine."

She shook her head.

I held out a hand. "Let's get you something to eat."

34

SYDNEY

When my feet touched the floor, I realized that I was wearing my UGGs booties... and my nightgown.

"Um."

"What is it?" Adam asked.

"I can't go to breakfast in my nightgown."

"Oh. I see." He seemed to be studying me with great consternation, trying to figure out what our options were.

"Wait here," he said. "My grandmother will know what to do."

"Okay," I said, but he had already dashed from the room.

I gazed around for my suitcase, but of course it wasn't here. It was in the future... along with the rest of my clothes. What had I been thinking? I'd known that going to the past was a possibility, so why hadn't I thought about what I was going to wear?

I pressed a hand against my forehead and shook my head.

How many people had to worry about what they were going to wear to the past?

It was a ridiculous notion. There were so many things I

could have… should have… would have… brought with me if I had been thinking.

Antibiotics. My cell phone and a battery pack. Blistex.

But I had not been thinking. Not in the least. It was like I just lost all my sense. It was somewhat logical to think that there could be some kind of magic involved in time travel. And if there was some kind of magic, it followed that a person might not have all their cognitive facilities about them during the process involved in time traveling.

There. I felt better now that I had a logical explanation for my lack of preparation.

Probably fifteen minutes later, Grandma Auclair came into the room with a stack of things in her hands.

"Good morning," she said.

"Good morning." I kept the blanket tightly around me, feeling self-conscious. "How is Mr. Auclair?" At least I hadn't lost all my manners and training.

"He's resting," she said. Then continued at my questioning look. "A bit of a headache, but he's going to be okay."

"His leg?"

"Just sprained."

"The doctor came then?"

"No," she said. "But when you live this far out with five children and raise them to hard teenagers, you learn a bit about medicine. Broken bones certainly."

"Of course," I said. Mrs. Auclair had a slight accent I hadn't noticed before. I couldn't quite place it.

"I've brought you some things to wear," she said, nodding toward the stack of clothes in her hands. "Come with me and I'll show you to the guest room."

"You're very kind," I said as I followed her from the sitting room, keeping the blanket wrapped around my shoulders.

"You have to be careful about spending time alone with Adam," she said.

"Why?" I imagined all sorts of things. Maybe he was dangerous. Or…

We started up the stairs. The blanket dragged on the floor behind me.

"You have your reputation to consider," she said. "If you aren't careful, you'll find yourself married to him."

"Oh," I said, not at all sure how I was supposed to respond to that.

I certainly couldn't tell her my first reaction. My first reaction was nothing less than shear happiness.

That told me that Grandma Auclair was right. I did have to be careful about spending time alone with Adam, but not for the reason she was thinking.

Simply because the thought of finding myself married to him was beautiful.

35

ADAM

S tanding up in the kitchen, I ate a piece of toast while I waited for Grandma to get Sydney settled in.

She'd told me to wait here, so that's what I was doing, even if it wasn't my first choice.

I didn't like being away from Sydney.

I paced from the window to the door and back again.

Paul sat at the table eating eggs and bacon.

"Where did you get that newspaper?" I asked.

"Miss Evette brought a stack of them." He looked up. Watching me for a minute before returning his attention back to the paper.

"Huh."

"You're welcome to sit down, you know," Paul said, turning the page of the newspaper.

I stopped pacing long enough to give him a quizzical look.

"Shouldn't you be outside doing something with the horses?" he asked.

"Shouldn't you be in class?" I asked.

"Not anymore," he said. "I've finished."

"What does that mean?"

"It means that Miss Evette can't teach me anything else."

With a noncommittal sound, I picked up a slice of bacon and started pacing again.

That was quite possible. My brother read all the time on his own. He could easily have outread his teacher.

"Adam," Grandma said, coming to the kitchen door. "Grandpa wants to talk to you."

"Why?" I asked.

"He's got his reasons," she said, looking at me over her spectacles. I might be thirty-one- years-old, but right at this moment, I may as well have been twelve.

"Yes ma'am." I grabbed a biscuit off the tray and took it with me as I followed her upstairs.

I did some mental calculations. Grandma had plenty of time to tell Grandpa about Sydney sleeping in the sitting room.

"Is Sydney in the guest room?" I asked with a glance in the other direction as we reached the second floor and headed toward Grandpa's bedroom. I'd never paid much attention to it, since I'd grown up here, but Sydney was right. The upstairs part of the house was something of a maze.

"She is."

Grandpa's room was closed and dark, the drapes keeping the sunlight out.

I followed her inside, sitting on one side of the bed while she sat on the other.

Grandpa was sitting up, propped against the pillows.

"Hello Grandson," he said.

"Grandpa. How are you?"

"I'll be better when I can get out of this damn bed." He glanced over at Grandma, and continued in a stage whisper. "But my captor doesn't allow it."

I put a hand over my mouth to hide a laugh. Grandma's stern expression told me she did not find this amusing.

"I'm sure you'll be up and about in no time."

He grunted noncommittally. "I understand that Sydney is back."

"She is," I said, not bothering to keep from smiling. They would find out soon enough that I was sweet on her.

Grandpa shifted to sit up straighter. Grandma jumped up to help him, adding another pillow behind him.

"There's something you need to know," he said, his voice sounding serious.

"About Sydney?" A sense of dread settled over me like a wisp of fog drifting in with the morning dew.

"Yes, actually." He took of his reading glasses and set them aside.

"What about her?"

Grandpa nodded to Grandma. She stood up, walked to the dresser, and came back with a leather book. She handed it over to Grandpa.

Grandpa held the leather book in his hands.

"I have reason to believe that you can't plan on her staying… here."

"What do you mean?" I asked, my heart sinking.

"This is a journal written in my brother's hand. He talks about his experiences with his wife."

"Rebecca." The woman who had traveled through time to marry my uncle.

"Yes. Rebecca."

"What does it say?" I wasn't sure I really wanted to know, but Grandpa seemed determined that I know.

"I'll let you read it," he said. "But I wanted to warn you that there's a very good chance Sydney won't be staying in this time for very long."

"I see." A simple response on the surface. But on the inside, I just might be going to be sick. Everything inside me rebelled. If I had anything to do with it, she would be staying in this time. Forever.

"I just want you to be prepared," he said.

"He doesn't want you to get hurt," Grandma said.

"Thank you. But I won't."

"Uh huh. Some things can't be avoided."

I stretched out my legs. Looked over at Grandma, but she had gone over to poke at the logs in the fireplace. The house had eight fireplaces. One in the main parlor. One in Grandma's sitting room. One in each of the six main bedrooms upstairs. There wasn't one in the guest room. That's probably why it had been designated as the guest room. Plus, there was the wood burning stove in the kitchen. My uncle had gone out of his way to make sure that whoever lived in the house stayed warm.

It was interesting that he just so happened to build enough bedrooms for all of us.

It took a lot of firewood to keep them all going. Paul and I had the job of chopping wood. Our younger brother was almost old enough to pick up his share of the wood splitting. He was already older than when Paul and I started using an ax, but being the youngest boy, we were all a bit overprotective of him.

"What are you trying to tell me?" I asked, leaning over, my elbows on my knees.

I took the leather book he held out to me. "Read this," he said. "then you will understand."

I thought about Sydney. I really didn't have time to read my uncle's journal right now. I had Sydney to think about. But I didn't dare tell Grandpa that.

"Alright," I said. "Thank you."

"Just be careful," he said.

"I will."

Grandpa nodded once to indicate he'd told me what he'd set out to say.

"That's it?" I asked, glancing from him to Grandma and back again.

"You can go now," he said as I stood up. "Just read the journal."

"Yes sir."

I took the journal to my bedroom, dropped it off at the nightstand, and wound my way around the maze of rooms that led me to the guest room.

36

SYDNEY

The guest room was sparsely furnished, but it had all the necessities. A small bed. A dresser. A pitcher of water. I wasn't sure if I was supposed to drink the water in the pitcher or wash with it. Probably both.

After a quick look around, I dropped the blanket off my shoulders and drew my nightgown over my head.

The dress Mrs. Auclair had given me was a dark gray wool dress with, thankfully, long sleeves. After I slid it on over my head, I saw that the hem reached the floor, but the dress was slightly shorter in front. Maybe half a dozen inches. Hmm. A high low dress. That was a surprise.

The dress had more than layer. There was the main layer, then an underskirt that purposefully peeked out beneath the hem in front and there was an outer layer that draped over the sides and down the back.

The material was soft and the skirt was full enough to make me feel feminine. I kept my Ugg boots on and used the hairbrush on the dresser to brush out my hair.

There was a little mirror attached to the dresser, but the glass was cloudy and I had to strain to see my reflection at all.

So… now. I stood in the middle of the room, turning side to side, allowing the skirts to swirl around me. What was I supposed to do now that I was here?

Grandma Auclair had warned me that I should be cautious about my reputation. How could I even have a reputation when no one knew me? I wasn't even from here. Not only not from here, but not even from this century.

But I would be cautious nonetheless, if for nothing else, out of respect for being in her home. I doubted Adam had to worry about his reputation. The double standard for that kind of thing—most things—was prevalent in the 1800s if what I knew about history was right.

Someone knocked on my door. Hoping it was Adam, I hurried to open it.

"Hi." It was Adam.

"Hi."

"Wow. You look beautiful."

I raised an eyebrow, but couldn't help the little glow of pleasure that warmed me from the inside out.

"Even more beautiful," he amended. "Can I come in?"

"I'll come out," I said, remembering what Mrs. Auclair had said. "There are no chairs in here." It was a good explanation, considering I came up with it in the spur of the moment.

"Very well," he said, holding out his arm for me. "We'll go downstairs to breakfast."

That sounded like a perfectly good idea since I hadn't eaten since… some time ago. I tucked my hand in the crook of his arm, a movement that was becoming quite familiar and natural.

With a smile on his lips, he looked down at me. Being a full head taller, he had to bend over a bit.

For just the briefest of moments, I thought he was going to kiss me. His gaze swept down to my lips, then back up to my eyes. Recognizing that look, my heart beat so hard I could hear the blood pulsing in my ears.

But a door closed just around the corner and the moment passed.

As we wove our way around the maze that led to the stairs, my heart was still pounding ninety miles an hour.

Still holding onto Adam's arm, I used my free hand for balance on the smooth wooden bannister as we walked down the stairs. Maybe it was the dress, but I had a feeling of being in the right place. It was a rather odd sensation considering the circumstances.

I should have felt out of place... out of my time... but on the contrary. I felt like I was right where I should be.

37

ADAM

*J*ust as I had been yesterday, I was impressed with Sydney's appetite. I found it utterly charming that she didn't pretend not to eat much.

I was also reminded that she probably had not eaten since yesterday.

"Can I ask you a question about the future?" I asked. "About this house?"

She nodded as she crunched into a strip of bacon.

"What do you want to know?"

"The house, it's still here? There?"

"Very much," she said. "Whoever built it did an excellent job. It's held up well through the centuries."

"My uncle," I said proudly.

"I know. Uncle Jack."

"Yes." I was inordinately pleased that she remembered my uncle's name. Of course, it helped that he had the same name as her Uncle Jack—in the future.

"Who lives in the house now?"

"No one," she said, stabbing up a forkful of eggs. "It's deserted."

I considered the implications of that.

"You spent the night there? Last night?"

"Yes." She shuddered as a slight shiver ran through her.

"By yourself. That must have been frightening."

"A little," she said, "but the house was locked securely."

"Still," I said with great admiration. "You're like a soldier."

She laughed. "Not really." She sipped her coffee and made a face.

"Except maybe when it comes to black coffee."

"I'm used to sugar and cr—milk."

"I'm sure we have some sugar," I said, standing up. "and milk. I'll be right back."

I found Frederick in the kitchen cutting up apples. I didn't even ask where they found such things as fresh fruit. "Do we have any sugar?"

"Of course," Frederick said. Frederick had been with the family since my uncle and aunt had built this house. Probably forty years. He even had his own room behind the kitchen.

He stopped what he was doing and pulled out a little glass jar full of the white sugar used only for special occasions. "Is this for the lady?"

"Yes. She likes milk in her coffee, too."

"Do you know? There was another lady who took cream and sugar in her coffee."

A little shiver ran up my spine. "Who was that?" I had a feeling I knew what he was going to say even before he told me.

"Your Aunt Rebecca. She's the only other lady I know who even drank coffee."

"I never really noticed that," I said. But of course, I had. I knew that my grandmother didn't drink coffee. And anytime she'd ever had ladies over to visit, they always had tea.

"Thank you," I said, taking the glass container of sugar and the little glass of milk back to the breakfast room.

Sydney was standing at the window, looking outside. Her back was to me, but I had a clear view of her profile.

She looked so very sad in that moment. Then I saw a single tear slip down her cheek.

Whatever had made Sydney sad?

Was it giving up her life in the future? I didn't know anything, of course, about that future, but she would have a life there. Family. Friends. Maybe even a husband.

The thought stopped me cold.

If Sydney already had a husband, I couldn't marry her. Not even if they were separated by time.

This changed everything.

I needed time to think about how this might work.

My gut was telling me that she could only have one husband, no matter if they were separated by time.

My heart broke a little with no more than the possibility that she might already belong with someone else.

38

SYDNEY

ensing someone behind me, I wiped a tear from my cheek and turned away from the window.

Adam stood there, holding two glass containers, one in each hand. He had a most perplexed expression on his face.

"Are you alright?" I asked.

"I was going to ask you the same thing."

"I'm okay." I moved forward taking the bowl of sugar from him, mostly just to have something to do. "Especially now that I have sugar for my coffee."

"And milk," he said, setting the little jar of milk on the table.

I took my time stirring the milk and sugar into my coffee. Then I made every effort possible not to make a face when I sipped what was essentially cold coffee.

I'd never caught on to the cold coffee trend. "Much better," I said.

"You don't like it," he said. "Something's missing."

I shook my head. "It's perfect."

"You suck as a liar," he said.

"Okay. Busted. It's good. It's just kind of cold."

He put both hands on the table and leaned forward as though suddenly inspired. "I can fix that."

"You don't have to…" I shrugged and met his gaze. "How?"

"Let me show you," he said, grabbing up the mug and holding out his other hand for me.

He led me through a door to the kitchen. It was interesting that the kitchen was separate from the breakfast room. The old house didn't exactly have an open floor plan. On the contrary, it had little nooks and crannies everywhere.

"Frederick," Adam said. "This is Sydney Brandt."

Frederick looked up from where he stood at what looked like a sturdy wood utility table with chunky legs in the middle of the room. In the future, I could see it being in someone's dining room. In the process of peeling apples, he had a bowl of peelings on his right and bowl of peeled apples on the other.

"It's a pleasure to meet you, Miss Sydney."

"Likewise."

"Frederick has been with the family since before the house was built."

"Part of the family, then," I said, smiling at Frederick. His face lit up. He was a thin man of average height and a beard hid any wrinkles he might have.

"Yes ma'am. What can I get you?"

"Do you think you could heat up her coffee?" Adam asked, holding out my mug.

"Of course," he said. "It would be my pleasure."

He poured my coffee diluted with sugar and milk into a small iron sauce pan and set it on top of a big wood burning stove next to the fireplace.

Not only was the stove burning wood, but an oversized fireplace burned brightly, too. Rows of potatoes lay tucked in the embers. I could only imagine that it took a lot of food to feed this large family along with their guests, myself included.

As I sat in the chair Adam brought over for me, I noticed

Frederick looking at me with curiosity. He looked away when I smiled at him.

I wonder. I just wondered what he was thinking. Did he see something about me that was unusual? Something that told him I was from the future. I shook my head. That would be highly unlikely and even if he did, it didn't really matter.

It wasn't exactly a secret that I was from the future. Adam knew. And that was all that mattered, wasn't it?

It only took a few minutes before Frederick was pouring my coffee concoction back into my mug.

"Careful not to burn yourself," he said, handing me the mug of steaming coffee.

He was right. I had to hold the mug carefully, by the top edges, to keep from burning my fingers. But even just one careful sip was blissfully good. It was no latte, but compared to what I'd had over last few days, it was wonderful.

"Thank you, Frederick," I said. "This is perfect."

Adam watched me with a little smile. "I can carry that for you," he said, holding out a hand. I placed the mug in his hand and as he carried it, somehow impervious to the heat, as went back out to the breakfast room.

"Now I know how to make you happy," he said, with a little smile, leaning close so no one else could hear.

I felt a little blush creeping over my skin. He had no idea.

I couldn't help but of so many ways he could make me happy. Just his gaze alone sent my heart into a frenzy.

39

ADAM

It was such a beautiful day, we opened the windows to let the house air out and let in some fresh air. The wind had quieted and the sun warmed the air.

Sitting on the back porch, Sydney and I could hear the rushing river from here.

"Are you sure you're okay?" I asked, thinking about seeing her crying earlier.

I wanted… needed to know more about her relationship status, but it didn't seem right to just come out and ask bluntly.

"I'm okay," she said, adjusting her skirts. "Really."

She'd been beautiful earlier, but now, wearing a dress, she was even more beautiful. Fortunately, I had never seen this particular dress before. Since occasions to wear dresses other than plain ones, were few and far between, my sisters had dresses they never wore. I was grateful I didn't have to purge any memories of one of my sisters in the same dress.

"You miss your… home," I said, skirting around the time travel issue.

"No," she said, with a little smile. "I don't. I really don't."

"But surely you think you will."

She shook her head. "Maybe."

"Besides hot sweetened coffee, what do you think you will miss the most?"

"Oh," she said. "You ask hard questions. Electricity and running water and maybe cell phones."

"I know about running water, but the other two not so much."

"You've heard of electricity," she said.

"Of course. But it's not something we have out here in any way."

She nodded. "Cell phones allow people to talk to anyone else who has one, even someone across the country."

"How does that work?"

"I don't know exactly. But everyone has one."

"Everyone?"

I looked out toward the tall rugged mountain peaks capped with snow. I hadn't missed my cell phone while I was here. Cell phones had gotten woven into our every day, every minute, every second life. But here... here... there was no need to be connected to a device.

"People are so attached to their phones, they might as well adhere them to their wrists."

"That sounds a bit uncomfortable," I said, trying to imagine it, but being horribly unsuccessful.

"Am I keeping you from doing something?" she asked.

"Probably." I grinned. "Tired of my company already?"

Her eyes widened. "Not at all. I just know that a ranch takes a lot of work."

"A valid observation."

"Maybe there's something I can do, too."

"You're a guest," I said, watching her reaction, but she just looked at me with those big beautiful eyes."

"I don't exactly have any other place to go," she said. "Not in this time."

I watched a couple of blue birds, landing only a few feet away, as they pecked at the ground searching for something to eat.

"While you're here, this is your home."

She nodded. Maybe that wasn't what she wanted to hear.

"What about in your own time? You have people who will miss you."

"My parents," she said. "But they have their own lives. They live in Florida and I hardly ever see them. I have friends at work who might miss me for a minute."

"No beau?"

"No what?"

"No one courting you?"

She looked at me blankly for a moment, then her lips curved into a smile. "No. No one courting me."

40

SYDNEY

*S*itting on the porch swing, my feet pulled up beneath me, I watched Adam as he chopped firewood.

He swung the heavy ax with what looked like ease, splitting the logs, leaving some in large pieces, chopping some into small pieces. Kindling, he said.

Straightening, he wiped his sleeve across his forehead and looked over at me. I still had the feeling that I should be doing something, even though he claimed I was a guest, but he insisted that I just be there. Called me his safety person or something like that.

Sitting and doing nothing other than being a safety person was a rather unusual activity for me. I was used to always having something to do. If I wasn't seeing a patient or charting, I was reading something. And to be honest, if I had my cell phone with me, I'd be on it right now. Doing something. Email. News. Texting. There was always something to do.

It was actually rather relaxing just sitting here, letting the soft breeze temper the warmth of the sun. If I hadn't been wearing a bonnet—one Adam grabbed from a peg near the door before we came outside—to shade my face, I was pretty sure I would have quickly gotten a sunburn.

Someone had planted a little spruce tree not far from the deck. Or maybe it had sprouted up naturally and they'd left it alone. Someday it would stand tall and provide a bit of shade for the deck.

An elk and her two babies frolicked a few yards away, over a knoll out of Adam's sight. Still, it was amazing to me that they didn't run. Not even the sound of the ax splitting the wood in two frightened them.

I could imagine living here with Adam. It was easy to pretend, even if just for a few minutes, that this was our home. We could have a family. I'd never thought much about having children, but now I could see it. I could imagine being a mother and Adam being the father of our children.

I could be happy. He'd asked about my relationship status. He'd gone about it in a roundabout way, an endearing kind of way, but still, he'd asked.

I wondered if he wanted me to stay. Maybe I should just come right out and ask him.

Maybe when he finished chopping wood, I would remind him that we needed to check his family Bible even I knew it wasn't going to tell us anything. I needed to look at it in the future, not now. That was where I was going to get my information.

Having made a decent sized stack of chopped wood and another one of kindling, Adam set the ax aside and came up to sit next to me.

Despite the cool weather, his skin glowed with a sheen of sweat. I'd spent most of my life around white color men who bought their firewood already chopped. That was certainly what Richard would have done, except that his fireplace was gas.

My ex-fiancé did not even clean his own home. He paid someone to come in once a week to do that.

At any rate, the difference between the two men couldn't have been greater. It was so great, in fact, that I couldn't even compare the two of them if I wanted to.

Adam looked up toward the sun.

"It's about time for lunch," he said.

"I guess it is," I said. I almost asked him if he was going to take a shower before lunch, but I remembered that there were no showers.

There was a well and there was a big fireplace in the kitchen. I would bet there was either a portable bathtub somewhere or a bathing room.

There were so many things I didn't know about life in the past, but I was going to have to learn them if I was going to stay in the past.

Did I even have a choice whether I stayed in the past or not?

If I decided that I wanted to stay here in this time, would I be able to?

"You're thinking about something awfully hard," Adam said.

I nodded. "I was just wondering about the whole time travel thing."

"What about it?"

I took a deep breath and jumped right into the deep end. "I was wondering if I have any choice over it."

"A valid question," he said. "Maybe it's best if you don't."

"Why would you say that?" I asked.

"Because I can't imagine the level of difficulty in trying to make a decision like that."

41

ADAM

The spring sunlight and dry air quickly dried the sheen of sweat that covered my skin. The blue sky was perfectly clear, not a cloud in the sky. The cap of snow on the mountain peaks reflected the sunlight.

The spruce trees and pines were showing new spring growth. It was a beautiful time of year. So much promise. Everything was new and fresh.

I had a stack of freshly chopped firewood ready for the day and a nice stack of kindling. Chopping kindling was underrated, but everyone used it. It was about time to chop down another tree. It was never too early to start getting ahead on the winter's supply of firewood.

Sydney sat on the porch swing, one foot tucked up beneath her, the other on the ground, rocking the swing with her furry boots.

She looked at me with a slightly stunned expression.

"What is it?" I asked. "What's wrong."

"Nothing," she said, looking down at her hands.

Then she looked up at me and smiled, but I saw the sadness in her eyes. I wondered if I was the one who had put that sadness in her eyes and if so what I could do to fix it. I didn't like her being sad, much less being the one to cause it.

When I held out a hand, she put hers in mine.

Her green eyes locked onto mine, seeming to search for answers to questions only she knew.

"If you do have a choice," I said softly. "I hope you decide to stay here. With me."

She smiled then and the glow returned to her skin.

I wanted to do whatever it took to keep that smile on her face.

"I asked my grandmother about the family Bible. She's bringing it out and will leave it in the sitting room."

She nodded slowly. "When can we look at it?" she asked.

"Now," I said. "Maybe. I need to wash up." I dusted my hands on my pants.

"Okay. I can wait out here."

"I'll be right back."

She nodded.

When I got to the door, I turned around and looked at her. The wind tousled her hair around her face. Her lovely green eyes framed with dark lashes watched me. When she smiled at me with those perfectly bow-shaped lips, my heart swelled with a mixture of happiness and… fear.

"Don't go anywhere," I said, one hand on the doorknob.

"I won't," she said, hugging her knees to her chest. "I'll be right here."

"Promise?"

"I promise," she said.

"I'm holding you to it," I said. I had a sudden, inexplicable fear of leaving her alone. A fear that she wouldn't be here when I got back.

I couldn't say that it was unfounded. She had vanished on me before. Would I always feel this way? Would I always worry that she was going to vanish? Surely it wouldn't always be this way.

Shaking off the fear, or at least putting it aside as best I could, I went to the washroom and filled a basin with water.

I felt good. Spending a good hour chopping wood was as good a workout as a man could ask for. It was a beautiful day. The sun was shining. The breeze was soft.

Using a bar of soap, I made a lather and rubbed it over my face. Shaving was always a calming activity. I just needed to relax.

Sydney would be sitting right there when I got back.

I'd have Frederick pack our lunch in a basket and we'd go on a picnic. Down by the river. Maybe we'd see an elk bringing her babies down to drink. Maybe Sydney would be more impressed by that than fish swimming upstream. I laughed at that. I thought with her being a Boston girl and all, she'd be a little easier to impress.

I stopped, before rinsing my razor. Maybe I'd take a pistol. Bears were out this time of year, too. Wouldn't hurt to have some protection. I was a strong man, but there was no way I could fight off a bear with my bare hands. I firmly believed that the legend of Daniel Boone killing a bear with his bare hands was nothing more than legend.

Cleanly shaven now, I changed shirts and went by the kitchen before I headed back outside.

Frederick was standing over a big cast iron skillet frying chicken.

"Would you pack a basket with enough food for two?" I asked.

Frederick grinned. "Of course. Shall I pack a bottle of wine as well for you and Miss Sydney?"

"Okay," I said, hiding my surprise. I don't know why I was surprised. It was no secret that Sydney and I were... What were we?

Courting, I decided. We were courting. And we'd be married as soon as I could talk her into it.

"Come back in about an hour," Frederick said. "I'll have the basket ready for you."

"Thanks, Frederick," I clapped him on the shoulder and grabbing a pretty green apple, headed back out toward the deck. Using the mud room door exit, I stepped outside.

An eagle, wings spread wide, gliding along, dipping low, looking for prey, must have seen me. He took off again, so close I could hear his wings flapping. So grand. I truly could not imagine living anywhere else.

This was my home. My heart swelled with pride and happiness.

I had everything I wanted now that I had found Sydney.

I turned to the right, toward the swing, and stopped.

The apple fell out of my hand, rolled along deck, and fell off the side.

The swing, still swaying, was empty.

42

SYDNEY

ulled into a sense of contentment, I closed my eyes and tilted my head up to face the sun.

My heart rate settled down to a normal rate. All Adam had to do was look at me and my heart went into overdrive.

I was content here… with Adam. I thought about my job at the mental hospital back in Boston. My patients. They would be in good hands with my interns. I had taught them well.

My parents might be a different story, but they did what they wanted to do. They hadn't asked me about moving to Florida. Just called when they got there and told me.

Granted, it was a little different situation, but they would get over it. I'd left a note in my car with their name on it and a request to return the car to the rental agency.

They would be okay.

Maybe this was my time to think about myself. To really put myself first and point my life in the direction I wanted to go. I'd always done what was expected. I'd gotten the college degrees. I'd taken the jobs. I'd been conventional.

But conventional, I'd only just learned, wasn't what made

me tick. Life had a tendency to get away from people. The years just kept passing by. If we did what others expected of us, where would they be when it was all over? Doing exactly what they wanted to do. Or maybe in all fairness doing what someone else expected them to do.

It was a never-ending rat race.

Granted, it wasn't like I just decided to up and move across the country to live at the ranch my Uncle Jack left me.

I went across the country to live at the ranch my Uncle Jack left me.

In another time.

In the past.

A cool wind swept over my skin and I *felt* the clouds suddenly blocking the sun.

I pulled the light shawl draped over my shoulders tighter.

The temperature must have dropped a full twenty degrees.

Maybe that's how it was in the mountains. Erratic weather. I'd heard of sudden storms up here.

I frowned. It wasn't just the weather that was different.

I heard… sounds. Sounds that I must be imagining.

A television in the background. Sounded like some kind of movie. The music was nice. A romance maybe.

I slowly opened my eyes and blinked.

It was dark now, not stormy, just twilight. Lightning bugs fluttered around the trees along the edge of the yard. The tall spruce tree next to the deck stood tall, its limbs brushing against the deck railing in the light breeze.

There were houses in the distance, lit up with bright lights. Cars traveling along highways in the valley, weaving around the sides of the mountains.

There shouldn't be any other houses. There shouldn't be any cars, much less cars roads carved into the side of the mountains. That came later.

My stomach dropped and I was suddenly lightheaded.

I closed my eyes, scrunching them together tightly and took a deep breath. The air was different. It smelled different. Like… popcorn?

Shaking my head as though I could shake off what I was seeing, I took another deep breath.

Something was wrong. Very wrong.

If I had gone back to my own time, then I should be alone. In a deserted `ranch house that had no electricity. There shouldn't be any other houses around. With electric lights.

And there certainly shouldn't be a television on.

No cars.

I slowly, cautiously opened one eye, then the other.

A sense of resignation settled over me.

I did not understand what had happened. Not even the faintest clue.

But there was one thing I did know.

I was not in the past.

More importantly, I was not with Adam.

43

ADAM

I looked for Sydney. I looked for any sign of her whatsoever. But my heart wasn't in it.

I already knew. She was gone.

She hadn't just wandered off.

She'd promised me she would be right there sitting in the swing where I had left her.

Paul even helped me looked. I knew what he was thinking. He was thinking that maybe she had wandered off to be eaten by a bear or a coyote.

I wasn't worried about that. There was always the possibility that an eagle could have swooped her up and if I hadn't known what had really happened to her, I might have entertained something like that. This was, after all, a wild untamed country.

My grandfather's words echoed in my head.

Sydney won't be staying in this time for very long.

Grandpa had known it.

After searching until darkness began to settle over the land, I went up to my room while the rest of the family gathered in the dining room for dinner. I hadn't eaten anything for lunch and didn't want anything now.

I lit a lantern and settled down at my desk to read my Uncle Jack's journal. I opened the leather-covered book and lightly touched the thick parchment.

Uncle Jack's handwriting was clear and easy to read. Very meticulous penmanship.

I should have read it when Grandpa gave it to me. He insisted that I read it, but no… I knew better.

I didn't think I had to listen to him. I had everything figured out.

I had Sydney.

Now I didn't have Sydney.

She had slipped out of my fingers and gone back to her time.

I opened the journal and started to read. Uncle Jack was an entertaining writer, but still, the first part was mundane and didn't really interest me. I just wanted to know about the time travel. But I forced myself to read every word so that I wouldn't miss anything.

This had happened because I hadn't done what I was supposed to do. My Aunt Rebecca had been from the future and she had stayed in this time period.

I looked up from the journal and stared out the darkened window.

Hadn't she?

Hell, I didn't even know. I had made all sorts of assumptions.

But Uncle Jack knew. Uncle Jack had written it all down. All I had to do was read it.

Grandpa had read it. If he thought it was worth my time to read, I should have listened to him.

Well, I told myself. I was reading it now.

When I got a third of the way into it, it got interesting.

Very interesting.

I learned things about my aunt and uncle that I never ever would imagined.

It was only when the clock downstairs chimed two times, that I realized I had been sitting here for hours. Reading.

With only a few pages left, I already knew what I had to do.

Feeling more optimistic than I had since I'd discovered Sydney gone, I saved the last few pages for later and, giving my eyes a rest, I wandered downstairs to get something to eat.

44

SYDNEY

I waited. Just sat there in the swing waiting for the complete darkness of night. An owl landed in the spruce tree next to the deck where I sat and set up a conversation with itself. I must have been sitting extraordinarily still.

They, whoever they were inside the house, turned off the television. And one by one the lights went off.

There were still lights on upstairs, but I couldn't sit here any longer, so I carefully stood up. I'd no more than stood up than a motion light came on.

My heart pounding dangerously in my chest, I sprinted across the deck and flattened myself against the wall so anyone looking out one of the upstairs windows wouldn't see me. I held my skirts tight against me to keep them from blowing in the wind.

I was so utterly confused. This made no sense to me.

None.

When I had first come here, the ranch house had been abandoned. Then I had been with Adam in 1879.

And now…

Now I had no idea.

Now the landscape itself was different from how I had ever seen it in either time. It was built up now with cars and houses everywhere.

The ranch was still the same, at least as far as I could tell from where I was standing.

Someone upstairs turned on music and a girl started singing along.

I recognized the song. Thank God.

That, at least, meant I wasn't in some kind of alternate universe.

The motion light went out. Finally.

I eased along the wall to the door. My skirt snagged on a rough place on the wall.

I wrapped my hand around the doorknob and held my breath, hoping it wasn't locked or even worse that there was no alarm as I slowly turned it.

The knob turned and as I pushed the door open, I slowly let out my breath. Moving slowly and silently, I stepped inside the house.

With the lights off, the house would have been a lot like it was in the past except for the humming of the refrigerator and the lights glowing beneath the cabinets in the kitchen.

The wall between the breakfast room and the kitchen had been knocked out, making it into one open modern—very modern—kitchen area.

I moved into the parlor where the grandfather clock stood... silent. The fireplace was out. It looked like gas logs had been installed.

I stopped in the middle of the foyer and looked up toward the stairs.

This was so very strange and I couldn't explain it.

I started to turn away, but then I heard footsteps coming toward the top of the stairs.

I stood very still and watched, Not daring to move as a teenager came to the top of the stairs.

Freezing, she looked right at me. She was late teens, shoulder-length hair, shorts and t-shirt. Bare feet.

I stood very still, not knowing what to do.

The girl slowly backed up, then I heard her take off running upstairs, her bare feet echoing on the floor.

I had no explanation for being here. I could be arrested for breaking and entering.

I hurried into the sitting room. It was much as it had been. Sort of. No cloths over the furniture. There were lamps now and an electric chandelier overhead. The fireplace was gas. But it still had a cozy feel to it.

Using moonlight as my guide, I went around to the sofa, looking for my handbag—the one I left in the future. I knew it wouldn't be there, but I needed to look.

It wasn't there, of course. Neither were Grandma Auclair's knitting needles.

I sat down on the sofa anyway. And there in the middle of the coffee table was the Auclair family Bible.

After a quick glance over my shoulder, I knelt down and slid it over to the edge of the table.

I heard two girls talking as they walked down the stairs.

"I know what I saw."

"Well, I don't see anyone."

"I'm telling you, I saw her. Long hair. Long dress. Just looking at me."

"You always did believe in ghost stories."

"It was her. It was the ghost of Sydney Auclair."

I didn't move a muscle. I don't think I even took a breath until I heard the two girls turn and go back upstairs.

Ghost?

Sydney Auclair?

What was going on here?

Looking down at my dress, I suppose that in the shadows, I could look a little like a ghost, but they had used my name.

Compelled to look inside the Bible, I picked it up and took it to a little writing desk in one corner of the room. I turned on the lamp, blinking at the shock of the bright light.

There was a flat desk calendar on the desk.

I just stared at it.

My brain could not compute.

May 25, 2045.

In case it was a heartless typo, I flipped ahead, but every page had the same year.

2045.

45

ADAM

I took a glass of whiskey with me and went outside through the French doors of my bedroom to stand on the balcony in the moonlight.

An owl set up a ruckus, then took off, obviously not wanting to share his space with me.

Clouds drifted over the moon, casting shadows across the ground. The tall mountains were hidden. If I didn't know they were there, I would have had no way of knowing.

The air was cool, but that was normal. I couldn't remember a night when the temperature didn't drop.

I set the glass on the banister and put both hands on the wood.

There was a storm coming in from the west. I could only see flashes of lightning with the low rumble of thunder, still far off.

Sydney could return. My uncle and grandfather had been half right.

But there were a host of things that had to come together to make it happen.

If this was the time she chose.

My Aunt Rebecca had chosen this time.

Everything had come together for her.

And after reading my uncle's journal, I now knew how he and Aunt Rebecca stayed together.

Both of them had made sacrifices.

Both of them had given up something they loved.

A coyote howled off to my left. A few minutes later a coyote off to my right answered.

I finished off my whiskey and listened as the two coyotes got closer and closer to each other. They, too, found a way.

Would Sydney make a sacrifice that would bring her back here to this time and keep her here?

She could very well have already chosen to go back to Boston. Back to her time.

If she did, I would never know.

But I would wait. I would give her every opportunity to make her way back.

And if she did come back, would I make the ultimate sacrifice that would keep her here?

I watched the storm a few more minutes as it got closer and closer.

The wind had picked up, howling around the corner of the house.

I went back inside and sat down at my desk.

I opened the journal and flipped to the last few pages. I'd already read them once, but I wanted to read them again.

I wanted to know more about Aunt Rebecca. She sounded a lot like Sydney. From the things Uncle Jack wrote about her, she was clearly a lot like Sydney. They were both from the future, so it made a lot of sense.

I tapped my fingers against the journal.

Aunt Rebecca had figured out about the time travel thing. She had figured out how to control it.

All I needed to do was get a message to Sydney. If I could

get a message to Sydney, she could use that information to get herself back to the past. If she wanted to.

There had to be a way.

I just had to figure out what it was.

Getting up, I walked over, refilled my glass with whiskey.

I didn't drink it this time. I just watched the amber liquid swirling in the glass as I turned the glass from side to side.

I paced back to the desk.

The rumble of thunder was getting closer. The storm would be over us in no time.

I stared at the journal.

Uncle Jack was the reason Sydney had come here. But if she couldn't stay, then what the point? There would be no point whatsoever in going to all that trouble to have her come here only to let her leave again.

Then, like a bolt of lightning, it hit me.

I knew what to do.

46

SYDNEY

I sat in the chair at the desk and opened the Bible.

2045.

I would have to think about that later. It was too surreal for my brain to absorb anyway.

Right now, I had to use what little time I had to look inside the Bible. Any minute, the police could arrive to take me away for breaking and entering.

They would probably put me in the insane asylum if I told then how I ended up here. The irony of that was not lost on me.

First of all, my name was in the book along with the wedding date I had seen before. 1879. That meant I had been there long enough to marry Adam. The question was how.

Next to my name was the number 1025. That was odd. No one else had a number. The dates beneath the number, where the dates of mine and Adams deaths could have been were smeared to the point of being illegible.

The number held no significance to me. It couldn't be an age. But it could be that something happened on October 25.

I sat back and considered. Perhaps it was a page number. I

quickly flipped to that page in the Bible and let the delicate pages fall to either side.

Yep. It had been a page number.

At first I didn't see it. I had, in fact, almost missed it.

Someone had written a note, printed small and carefully right there on one of the pages of the Bible in the center of the book next to the margin. Someone just flipping through or maybe even reading casually wouldn't see them. I leaned forward and read.

SYDNEY,

Put the key in the grandfather clock. Then in the second between the lightning flash and following thunder, turn the clock back one hour.

Meet me in 1879.

Adam

IT WASN'T much of a note, but it had lasted all these years. It had lasted for centuries.

The key.

A secret code. The key that *could* though not necessarily *would* send a person through time.

That's what Adam had given me.

I had the clock.

Now all I needed was the key.

Moving quietly, I went into the parlor and looked up into the face of the silent grandfather clock.

According to the note, there should be a key inside.

I opened the little glass door to find a key in the lock.

Well. I took a step back.

It couldn't be that easy. Could it?

Maybe it was.

So now I had the key.

All I needed was the storm.

What were the odds of that happening?

I heard someone walking upstairs. Heard voices.

Even if there was a storm and I had the key, it might not matter unless it happened pretty soon.

I couldn't stay here.

I couldn't stay here and I had nowhere else to go.

I was in effect, quite simply, lost in time.

47

ADAM

Two weeks later

It had been the longest two weeks I had ever spent. Time moved more slowly, it seemed, with a broken heart.

And the weather seemed to mock me. The days were unbelievably beautiful and sunny. Not a cloud in the sky. The nights were just cool enough that I longed for Sydney to spend them with me. Sit in the porch swing and snuggle under a blanket beside me, listening to the night noises.

Barely sleeping, I woke early in the mornings and haunted the house at night until collapsing onto my bed with exhaustion.

I had enough firewood chopped and neatly stacked to last through the summer and even into the winter.

I hardly spoke to anyone. Not my grandparents. Not my brothers or my sisters.

I spent my days in the fields herding the cattle. The cows

didn't ask questions and I wasn't obligated to explain myself to them.

Grandpa was up and moving around again. I caught glimpses of worried glances from both of my grandparents whenever we crossed paths.

Fortunately, it was a big house.

Today was a bit different though because everyone had saddled up to go into town. Into Whiskey Springs for supplies. They were even taking two empty wagons with them. First trip into town since the first snowfall.

I couldn't bear to go. Not without Sydney.

So I found myself alone in the house. Alone to pace out my misery.

Unfortunately it followed me with every step I took.

I finally made use of the time by settling into the study to catch up the household accounts. There wasn't much to do, but there would be lots of entries when the family came home today.

Lots of withdrawals to enter into my ledgers.

I had been planning to go. To take Sydney. I would have bought her dresses appropriate to this time. I didn't care if she wore pants, but a girl needed a dress now and then and I was determined that my girl have the best.

As I worked, night fell. Realizing it was dark now, I looked up from my desk, setting my pen aside and putting a stopper in the inkwell.

Since my hands were covered with ink, I got up and, taking my lantern with me, walked through the parlor to the back washroom.

It took a few minutes of heavy scrubbing to get most of the ink off my hands.

While I scrubbed, I looked in the mirror. I hadn't shaved in the two weeks Sydney had been gone. I looked like a mountain man.

I couldn't go around looking like this. I'd scare people.

No wonder they'd been looking at me all funny.

I felt immensely better after I got cleaned up. Maybe I'd even go upstairs and put on a clean shirt.

Heading upstairs, I walked through the main parlor. For some reason, I stopped in front of the clock and stared blankly its face.

I'd done this so many times since I had read about the clock in Uncle Jack's journal. The key was right there in the lock.

Sydney was supposed to turn the key. During a thunderstorm. But how was she supposed to turn the key when it was right here? When it was in the past?

I refused to feel hopeless about it.

It had to be fate. It just had to be.

Otherwise, why had she even come here?

I held tight to my belief that she would find a way back.

When I heard a rumble of thunder in the distance, my heart leapt for joy.

Not that I could do anything with it, but still… there was a storm.

And I had the key.

48

———

SYDNEY

I slept on the sofa in the sitting room.

It was a risky thing to do since I could be found at any time.

But I had my reasons.

First of all, I had fallen asleep on the sofa and woke up in the past before. So that was a possibility.

Second, I was exhausted and I had no other place to go.

I took it as a good sign that I needed to sleep. Those girls had called me a ghost. And I admitted to myself that I was more than a little bit disturbed by that.

So since ghosts did not sleep, I was relieved that I could. My new mantra. *I am not a ghost.*

I slept lightly, probably only dozed, so I woke at the first indication that anyone was up and about.

I slipped outside and found a place to hide at the side of the house behind a big spruce tree.

I would just stay here until I figured out what it was I was supposed to do.

The traitorous weather was lovely. Blue skies. Not a cloud in the sky.

Even if I could get to the clock, there was no storm.

To say that it was a long morning was an understatement.

I watched the progress of the sun.

As I sat here, I came up with no solutions to my predicament. I had gone from the past to the future.

I didn't know if I could get back to my own time even if I wanted to.

I exhausted my brain going around and around, searching for some kind, any kind, of solution until finally I dozed.

It was sometime after the sun passed the Noon point that I felt a splash of rain on my face. I realized then what woke me. Thunder.

Thunder.

There was a storm.

I had to get inside the house. To the clock.

To wait for the lightning.

I stood up, wiped the dirt off my dress as best I could.

I was going to be soaked. I could go into the house looking like a drowned rat in a long dress.

I stood there until the storm was over me, warring with myself, neither side winning.

It was an impossible situation.

I had to get back to Adam. I didn't even care about getting back to my own time. I just wanted to get back to Adam.

There was no solution. None.

I knew how to travel through time, at least I think I knew. I had the code. But what time would I go to?

Whoever would have guessed that I would go to the future?

As the storm raged overhead, I went around to the back door. Maybe I could just slip inside. Get to the clock.

Maybe the family had gone upstairs to take a nap.

I felt an urgency surging through me.

It was now or never. I could not keep living outside in the yard.

Now or never.

The words kept running through my head, pushing me forward.

By the time I got to the back door, I was soaked just as I had predicted.

When I hesitated, a bolt of lightning crashed right there, almost touching me.

"Okay. Okay. I get it."

Turning the door knob, I slipped in through the back door, through the mudroom.

Through the empty kitchen.

So far so good.

The clock chimed the hour. Two o'clock.

I was being pulled toward the clock and pushed by the lightning.

I reached the opening to the parlor.

The first thing I noticed was that the gas fireplace was on. Warm cozy flames.

Then one by one, seven people looked up from where they sat on the couches—a big sectional and another couch in front of the fireplace. Five teenagers and two adults.

They were just sitting there. Using their electronic devices. Electronic devices I didn't recognize. Something between an iPad and a laptop.

There was no television in the room.

What kind of future was this?

I'd heard a television last night. But today… today they were all sitting together. Not making a sound.

It was so… undysfunctional.

I was pretty sure I had lost my sanity. I was even making up words. I could lose my license to treat others with mental disorders for that.

They all sat so perfectly still. Just looking at me.

Like I was a ghost.

Not just any ghost, but a soaking wet ghost dripping water all over their floor.

I opened my mouth to speak, but nothing came out.

I didn't know what to say.

Taking a deep breath, I closed my eyes.

49

———

ADAM

In the second between the lightning flash and following thunder, turn the clock back one hour.

I had the statement memorized.

Sydney was supposed to do it. Right?

Had I made assumptions about things I knew nothing about?

I stood in front of the grandfather clock. The little glass door open. Staring at the key.

The scent of fresh daisies mixed with the scent of the storm.

Lightning flashed all around me and rumbles of thunder shook the house. This was the storm of all storms.

I hoped my family had decided to stay in Whiskey Springs for the night. They did not need to get caught in this storm.

It occurred to me that I should go look for them, but it was a passing thought that came and went quickly.

Standing in front of the clock, my heart pounding like a race horse, I reached up and grasped the little key.

How could one little key determine lives?

A bolt of lightning flashed across the room.

This was it.

This was the moment.

I turned the key back one hour as the thunder bellowed overhead.

Had I been too slow? There was hardly any time between the lightning flash and the thunder.

Everything went quiet.

There was a distinct possibility that I had not considered until this very second.

I may have traveled through time.

But nothing looked different. Everything looked the same. The fire crackling in the fireplace. The darkness on the other side of the dark blue velvet curtains.

The fresh daisies on the table next to the grandfather clock.

I slowly took a deep breath, then slowly let it out.

Nothing had happened.

I closed the door to the clock.

Then I had the craziest thought. I'd have to reset the time. Like that was important.

I turned around.

And blinked.

Sydney stood there. She was wearing the same dress she had worn two weeks ago.

Her fists clenched at her sides. Her eyes tightly closed, causing her face to scrunch up.

I bit my lip to keep from laughing out loud.

It wasn't funny. But I was overcome with emotion. Happy emotion.

"Sydney," I said.

"I'm not a ghost," she said softly.

Closing the distance between us, I put my hands on her elbows.

When she opened her eyes and saw me, she swayed a bit. Glanced at the room behind me.

"Adam?" Her voice was filled with wonder and disbelief.

I pulled her to me, cupping the back of her head with one hand and wrapping her around the waist with my other. She was drenched and getting me soaked and I didn't care one bit.

Her breath hitched and I realized she was crying.

"Don't cry, my love," I said. "You're here. You're here and I'm never going to let you go."

"How?" she asked. "How do I stay?"

I put a finger beneath her chin and slowly nudged her until she met my gaze.

"You made the sacrifice to leave your time," I said. "To come to the past. Now I have to make one."

"What?"

Her hair was soaked, her clothes were soaked and she was trembling a little.

"Have you ever heard of Montana?"

"Of course," she said, her brows furrowed.

"Let's get you into some dry clothes and I'll explain everything."

I took her hand and led her upstairs to her room.

The grandfather clock chiming the hour echoed through the house.

I missed a step and looked over my shoulder.

The clock had reset itself.

EPILOGUE

Sydney

I rode a horse, a dapple gray, and Adam drove the covered wagon pulled by two sorrels.

They probably wondered what they had done to deserve such treatment, but once we got to Montana, they could go back to being regular, self-respecting saddle horses.

Half a dozen cattle followed along beside us.

Two guides rode ahead of. No telling how much money this trip was costing. But no one seemed to care. It was sort of like the 1879 version of traveling by private jet.

Adam glanced over and winked at me.

I smiled. We had been married this morning in what most people would call a hasty wedding.

I didn't care. His family had been there. There had been more than a few tears. The Auclair family was close. For Adam to walk away from them was a significant sacrifice.

That was how it worked. I gave up my time and he gave up his home.

We would make a new home for ourselves in Montana.

Build our own ranch from the ground up. It was daunting and exciting all swirled into one.

The few people who knew about the time travel had figured out that the house, maybe along with the clock, was a time portal. And somehow it was in my blood starting with the Aunt Rebecca I hadn't met, much less known I had.

The only way to be certain I didn't travel through time again was for us to leave here.

I certainly didn't want to end up in the future again. They had called me a ghost and to them I guess I was. I didn't know why they thought they knew me, but there were some things that were well enough off remaining a mystery.

Adam and I were on our way to Montana.

And finally, I would meet Uncle Jack.

The man who had changed my life.

"We should stop for lunch soon," Adam said.

"Already?" I looked up at the sun. "It's not Noon."

"It's okay," he said.

I tried to calculate how long we had been riding. Learning to gauge time without a watch was a process. Adam promised to get a pocket watch once we got settled.

"Are you hungry?" I asked. Adam was always hungry.

"Of course. But that's not why I want to stop."

I looked over at him with a raised eyebrow.

"I want to stop so I can kiss you," he said.

I grinned to myself.

I was having a good life.

And it all began in 1879.

Keep Reading for a preview of Midnight Storm...

PREVIEW MIDNIGHT STORM

Prologue

*D*aniel picked up the two-month-old kitten and held it close to his chest.

The kitten mewed and stuck its soft little claws in his arms.

"You can take him home," Vaughn said, opening a big leather trunk in the dusty attic.

Daniel's eyes widened with delight, then he stuck out his lip.

"I can't," he said. "My mom will have my hide."

Vaughn smiled.

To Daniel, at the tender age of eight, Vaughn Becquerel was beautiful. And Daniel was smitten.

But Mama said she was too old for Daniel. At least forty.

Daniel didn't believe it, much less care.

Didn't matter though.

Vaughn was married to Mr. Jonathan.

Mr. Jonathan Becquerel had fought in Vietnam and Mama said Daniel should be nice to him. Said he had the PTD.

Whatever that was. Mr. Jonathan seemed nice, but Mama seemed to be afraid of him.

"It's ok," Vaughn said. "You can play with him when you're here."

"Really?" Daniel's eyes lit up. He hugged the kitten even tighter.

"Sure thing," Vaughn said. "You can even name him if you want to."

He looked down at the little kitten, purring now in his arms. It had the longest whiskers Daniel had ever seen. "Whiskers," he said. "I want to name him Whiskers."

"Then Whiskers it is," Vaughn said. "Now set Whiskers down for a minute. I want to show you something."

Daniel set the kitten down on the floor next to him, but kept one hand on him.

"What is it?" he asked, running a hand over the top of the dusty trunk.

"Drumsticks," Vaughn pulled out a set of what looked like well-worn drumsticks.

"Cool," he said. "Are they from a famous musician?"

Vaughn smiled. "No," she said. "They're from a little drummer boy. Back in the Civil War."

"What kind of war was that?" he asked, keeping his eyes on the drumsticks as he ran his fingers over the kitten's little ears.

"You'll learn about it in school soon enough," she said. "But it was a very very long time ago. And these belonged to a little soldier about your age."

"No way," he said, looking at Vaughn now. "You know I'm only eight-years-old, right?"

Vaughn nodded. "I know. But this little boy lied about his age." She lowered her voice to a whisper as though someone might overhear.

"Was it Mr. Jonathan?" Daniel asked, looking over his shoulder.

Vaughn laughed now. "No. But the little boy was probably brave like Jonathan."

Brave. Not crazy. Daniel would have to tell Mama that about Mr. Jonathan.

"Would you like to hold them?"

"Can I?" Daniel asked, forgetting the kitten for the moment and clasping his hands together.

"You can," Vaughn said. "But you have to remember something."

"What's that?" Daniel asked. Whatever it was, he'd remember it.

"You have to remember that no matter what you do, you have to be brave."

"Like fight in a war?"

"That's one thing," Vaughn said. "But it's not the only thing."

Daniel nodded.

Vaughn placed the drumsticks in Daniel's hands.

They were rough with lots of use. And much heavier than he'd expected.

"Can I play with them?"

"You can," she said. "and if you like them, you can keep them. On one condition."

Daniel experimented with the feel of the heavy wooden drumsticks. He tried to imagine an eight-year-old being in a war. Playing the drums.

"What's that?"

"It won't make sense right now," she said. "But you'll understand later."

"I'll understand," Daniel said. "Mama says I'm old for my age."

Vaughn smiled again.

"You have to promise me that you'll follow your heart."

Daniel tapped one of the drumsticks against his palm and scrunched up his face.

"Ok," he said. "I'll try." Vaughn was right. He didn't understand."

"Good enough," she said.

"Now take Whiskers and your drumsticks and go play out back 'til your Mama gets here to pick you up."

Daniel put his drumsticks in his back pocket and picked up his new kitten.

But instead of leaving, he put his arms around Vaughn and hugged her.

"I love you, Vaughn," he said.

"I love you, too Daniel," she said. "Now get out of here before I put you to work."

Daniel turned and skipped across the attic floor, dodging old boxes and discarded furniture.

He wouldn't mind staying and helping Vaughn, but he knew that Mr. Jonathan would be coming up soon to look for her.

And Daniel erred on the side of caution that his Mama might be right about him being a bit crazy.

Chapter 1
October 2021

DANIEL STOOD in front of his telescope and adjusted the lens. The tripod, secure in the soft dirt, settled a little more as he made adjustments.

He reached into his backpack next to it and pulled out a ten-millimeter lens. Slid it into the eyepiece.

It was a Hunter's Moon tonight.

And Daniel had a perfect view of one of the moon's mountain ranges.

An owl that had been watching him, fluttered in the oak tree behind him. Called out a questioning hoot.

Daniel's dog, Biscuit, paced a wide circle around him.

Biscuit was a two-year-old big black gangly dog. He'd been a stray when Daniel had gotten him from the pound. And he'd spent his few months chewing up everything from Daniel's running shoes to his ties.

For some reason, the dog seemed to have an affinity for Daniel's clothes, especially his work clothes.

But Biscuit had grown out of his chewing stage, then gone through his running phase, and was currently seemed to be in a pacing phase.

The last couple of times, when Daniel was out moongazing, the dog had just sat at his heels, with what looked like boredom.

But not tonight.

Tonight Biscuit was restless.

Maybe it was the cold weather.

Sometimes October in Mississippi was chilly, like tonight. But sometimes it was quite warm. This was actually the first time Daniel had brought Biscuit out in the cold.

The scent of honeysuckle was strong, but refreshing. It muted the murky scent of the Mississippi River not too far from here.

In his high-rise apartment building near downtown Dallas, Daniel rarely had the chance to be out in nature. Besides, the view of the moon out here as so much better than the view he got from his balcony. Too many lights in Dallas.

But this month's hunter's moon had coincided with Daniel's fall break and since he had no other obligations at the time, Daniel had thrown a few things into a dusty duffle bag and taken a road trip. Been drawn almost automatically to the area outside of Natchez.

He had fond memories of this area from his childhood.

He'd spent his summers near here. Those three months out of every year when his father would drop him off at his mother's house and head out of the country.

To this day, Daniel didn't really know how his mother felt about those summers. His father, a university professor, just like Daniel, spent his summers volunteering in various less fortunate countries—places one couldn't take a youngster.

Daniel had inherited his father's inclination for science, but instead of going in the medical direction, Daniel had gone with math.

Numbers didn't lie. Daniel found comfort in that.

When nothing else in his life had made sense, numbers had.

But the real kicker was the Daniel's mother had her own busy life. Daniel had never been privy to his parents' conversation and they remained a mystery to him.

His mother had been an attorney who spent most of her waking hours at the office there in Natchez.

That gave Daniel months of freedom that most boys didn't get.

Still. When his mother came home at night, Daniel was expected to be there and was required to account for how he spent his days.

Most of his time was spent at the Becquerel's home not far from this very spot. The owner, Vaughn Becquerel, had taken Daniel under her wing.

Daniel rested his eyes a moment and scratched Biscuit's ears.

He never had found out his mother's connection to Vaughn Becquerel. When he was old enough to think about asking his mother, she'd changed the subject.

The dog whimpered a bit.

"What's wrong boy?" Daniel asked. "We won't stay much longer."

There was a dampness in the air that Daniel hadn't expected and he didn't want to risk getting caught in the rain with his gear.

Putting a hand on the telescope, Daniel tried to remember whether or not he'd fed Biscuit. Surely he'd remembered.

But what other explanation did he have for Biscuit's uncharacteristic behavior?

Reaching into his jacket pocket, he found one of the dog bones he kept there for their trips to the park.

Biscuit raced over, took it from Daniel's hand and sat down to chew on it. That would hold the dog, at least.

Daniel rubbed his hands together. The moon went behind the clouds in what a few minutes ago had been a cloudless sky.

There was no accounting for weather, no matter how many times he checked the forecast.

In the unexpected darkness, Daniel bumped his telescope, sending the aim through the trees into the darkness.

Out of habit, maybe superstition, he peered through the telescope lens.

Adjusting the focus, he saw a light in the distance.

A lantern, a bright lantern, right there in his range of vision through the telescope.

Daniel looked up, but couldn't see anything other than darkness with his naked eyes.

He looked back down, focusing his sight through the lens.

He tilted the scope enough to better see the light.

He was looking at the veranda of a house

Again, he pulled back and looked into the darkness. He should be able to see the light from here.

Maybe. Maybe not.

Looking through the lens again, he zoomed out a bit.

There were four people sitting there in the light of the lantern. Three young men and a young lady.

He could barely see the lady's silhouette. Not enough to make out more about her than she was young.

He had a decent look at the men. One was sitting on a rocker facing the girl. Another had one foot propped on the railing of the veranda. And the other stared into the darkness. Toward him actually.

Daniel lifted his head, put his hands on his hips and looked around him into the darkness.

As far as he could tell, he was looking toward the old Becquerel place. It was supposed to be deserted.

Maybe some college students had picked the deserted house to have a Saturday night soiree. As a college professor, Daniel was quite familiar with the creativity of college students in finding places to hang out.

Curious now, he looked through the scope again.

From what he could tell, the young people were having a lively conversation. He didn't see any beer bottles or joints or anything other than a couple of glasses of water sitting on a little wooden table.

He stood up, rubbed his eyes.

What he did see, however, was perplexing to say the least.

The men were wearing what looked like formal attire.

The young lady was wearing a long, full dress.

He looked again.

Maybe they'd been to a prom or some such.

But this was October.

A Fall Formal?

They could easily be high school students. Maybe college. he really couldn't tell from here.

As he watched, one of the men opened the door and went inside the house.

The house was obviously deserted. He didn't see any other lights other than the one lantern.

It was one thing for them to sit out on the veranda. It was another entirely for them to go inside the house.

He ran a hand through his hair and groaned.

So much for a quiet, peaceful evening watching the moon.

Chapter 2
October 1860

BEATRICE EDWARDS STOOD at her bedroom window and watched the three men parrying and lunging below.

Her two brothers and her third cousin were training for battle. At least that's what they called it.

Beatrice wasn't sure there was even going to be a war. Surely the men weren't that stupid.

Her brother, John, lopped off one of her mother's roses.

All three men froze. Then all broke into laughter while looking toward the house.

If Mama had seen that, they'd already have their ears boxed.

Her cousin, Wilford caught sight of Beatrice watching them and grinned up at her.

Beatrice dropped the emerald velvet curtain and took a step back.

Wilford needed no encouragement. He already believed that Beatrice was going to marry him.

Unfortunately, he wasn't the only one.

"Beatrice," her brother John called up. "Come down and join us."

Beatrice pretended not to hear.

"She doesn't want to come down here," her older brother Sam said.

Considering the nonsense of the war, Sam was the sensible one. Sensible Sam. That's how she thought of him.

But even a sensible man obviously could get caught up in the anticipation of the chance to kick some Yankee butts.

Beatrice could have joined them. In fact, just a few months ago, she would have.

But she was grown up now and no longer played with the boys.

Mama had started making her wear long dresses when she'd turned seventeen.

"It's time to turn this little ragamuffin into a lady," she'd said.

Beatrice had resisted at first.

She so enjoyed traipsing about the countryside with her brothers.

But putting on dresses had changed things.

For one thing, Wilford had started looking at her differently.

Beatrice didn't particularly like Wilford, but still, it was hard not to be flattered by the attention.

For another thing, Beatrice actually liked wearing the dresses.

Right now, in fact, she was wearing a pretty mink colored dress over wide hoops.

The skirts swayed with every movement.

It had taken some practice to learn how to manipulate the hoop skirt, but Beatrice was a fast learner.

All in all, Mama had been quite patient with her. Living out in the country had allowed her freedom that she wouldn't have had in the city.

The freedom to roam with her brothers. Sensible Sam, two years older, and John, two years younger.

But those days were over.

She was definitely a lady now.

Chapter 3

DANIEL TOOK a flashlight from his backpack, called Biscuit, and started the trek over to the house.

It wasn't that far.

In fact, he'd played out here in this area between the house and the river countless times.

He knew that there was a little gully off to his right and a fallen tree across it.

He knew that if he climbed up that tree and climbed up into the oak tree next to it, he could see the river for miles. He could also see the house and the dirt driveway leading to it.

He'd climb up and watch for his mother's Mercedes when it was time for her to come and pick him up.

When he saw her turn into the driveway, he could be down the tree, to the house, and inside the back door before she parked in front of the house.

He smiled to himself.

He'd been quite the little rebel back then for such a little tyke.

Something slithered in the bushes and he jumped before he caught himself.

Biscuit ignored it and kept walking.

Daniel kept his light down. He wanted to assess the situation before he made his presence known.

There were too many things he didn't know. For all he knew, these kids had a right to be here.

As he neared the house, he listened for signs of the kids.

The clouds had drifted over the moon now, so it was just as well that wasn't trying to see anything through his telescope.

He reached the edge of the trees where the area opened up around the house.

The clouds shifted enough that he could see the house.

It was dark just like he expected.

But there was no one there on the veranda.

He stood there a minute. Biscuit sat next to him, looking up at Daniel questioningly.

Daniel looked over his shoulder. He had not gotten turned around.

Had he?

He clicked off his flashlight and started making his way around the side of the house.

It had grown up with high grass and brambles over the years.

When Vaughn had lived here, she'd employed a gardener who'd kept things looking immaculate.

He remembered roses and daisies and all sorts of flowers in different colors.

She'd told him that she liked to keep it the way it had been back when the house was in its prime.

Daniel hadn't understood, of course, at the time how a house could have a prime, but he did now.

The house was in a downhill spiral at this point.

He assessed the windows as he passed. Though the light was low, he could see that there was no broken glass.

The house could still be salvaged. It was far from too late. He'd see about going inside tomorrow while he was still here.

Then he caught himself.

He wasn't here to buy an old house.

He was just here to gaze at the moon.

The tides of the moon had been known to do funny things.

Had the full moon called him here?

Daniel hadn't had any particular inclination to come here before this morning. In fact, he hadn't really even thought about it this morning. He'd just packed his things, got in the car and started driving as though he'd planned to come here all along.

Just like his father had done all those years. But his mother lived in Florida now. Had made her money and retired.

Daniel didn't know much about his mother. But he was ok with that. He had his life in Dallas.

He was content.

He stopped in front of the house.

It was obvious that no one was here.

Maybe the kids had seen him coming and had left before he got close enough to see them.

He'd just go back, get his telescope, and go to the hotel.

There was nothing to see here.

Keep Reading Midnight Storm…

Kathryn Kaleigh writes sweet contemporary romance, time travel romance, and historical romance.

kathrynkaleigh.com